The Allot

By

Jethro Le' Roy

Dalyn Publishing
Dalyn House
Lower Hillmorton Rd
Rugby CV21 4AE

Enquiries and submissions:
dwfurlong@talktalk.net

Also available in the series:
The Allotment….Continued!
The Allotment…..Reprisal!

By the same author under his Dave Furlong pen name :
John Slater: The Journey
John Slater: The German Job
And the Oh Grumps! Series of childrens books

The Allotment!

It was a nice sort of day.

   The sort of day that made you want to get out of the house. Take a walk with the dog. Mooch about the garden. Wash the car. Anything, short of taking the wife shopping, was preferable to staying in the house.

   Just lately, the house was feeling like a prison. I don't mean it had bars at the window or guards walking up or down, it was just…. Oh, I don't know, restricting, claustrophobic…. Whatever. I just knew I had to get out from under its roof for a while. Retirement sucked.

Funnily enough I had been looking forward to my retirement. Most of my working life had been spent away from home. This home….the one that had been ours for the last 35 years. The one that I had proudly made the final mortgage payment on the day that I turned 60 years young.

The house that was more a home to my wife Lynne, our three children – now all living in their own homes – and a fluctuating number of Yorkshire terrier dogs than me.

I had been a long distance truck driver. First in the UK then Europe and finally the Middle East. Hard work with long periods away from home.

I had gone from being an employed driver to being my own boss. The rewards for making my own decisions were good. The penalty was more and more time away. Two or three nights a week on UK work. All week as I drove all over Europe. The Middle East work was a minimum of six weeks away.

But, I had kept at it. Made good money. Then, because of a simple eye infection, I had to make an unprecedented career change and became, of all things, a journalist. A transport journalist no less.

I had been good at that too. But, even that kept me away from home. European press jollies to test drive the latest trucks, vans or engines. Weeks spent on continuous road development testing of trucks, engines and drivelines.

So, as I approached my sixty fifth birthday, I was looking forward to retirement.

Spend time with my long suffering wife, Lynne. Help the kids. Make a start on the To Do list of things that needed doing around the house.

Yeah, well. It didn't work out exactly how I planned. Lynne had ruled supreme whilst I was away. And, didn't take kindly to me interfering with her routine.

My son and two daughters had married and were living their own lives. With varying degrees of success. My son and elder daughter had both been divorced, produced three children each and were routinely either starting or ending new relationships.
My youngest daughter was happily married and expecting her first.

The upshot, as I quickly began to realise, was that I was not really needed at home. Things were ticking over nicely. Just as they always had without me. I was, in fact, just about tolerated.

Don't get me wrong. We still loved each other. Still got along. Laughed, loved, held hands. But the house was undisputedly hers and I had yet to find my place, my role in the day to day functioning and routines.

I was allowed to repair, decorate, hump furniture about, tend to the garden and manly stuff like that. But, anything else and I got the impression that the house would exist quite happily whether I was there or not.

I was, in fact, beginning to resent the house. Started to think of it as The House like it was a separate entity or something. I think The House resented me as well.

Why else would it resist my efforts to repair, improve and beautify it? Why did it need to shrug off my newly pasted wall paper like a split banana skin? Why did it contract and make my woodwork appear to be less than straight? Why make my new electrical connections go bang and explode when something was plugged in? It wasn't me so it must be the house, right?

Obviously, something needed to be done before I did something drastic. Like sell up and find a new house. One that would love me like this one loved Lynne. One that would accept me unconditionally as a valued and welcome member of the household. I tried to ignore the little voice in my head that said moving house wouldn't make a difference.

The solution that saved my sanity was a simple encounter with a near neighbour in the till queue at Aldi.

Like most men, I like to be in and out when shopping. As quickly as possible. During the last year or so, I had been trusted enough to do the shopping by myself. But, I had to stick to The List.

The List told me what to buy and what not to. Except in very special circumstances, I wasn't allowed to deviate from it. It wasn't total freedom but it was a start.
Anyway I was standing in line and behind a thirty something aged guy who lived just up the road from me. We weren't best pals or anything. More along the lines of a "Good Morning" and innocuous stuff like that.

He turned around as I took my place in the eight person queue behind the only working till. He nodded his head and raised his eyes to the heavens. Manly chitchat shorthand. Translated as "All these customers and only one till. I don't normally do this but I decided to help the wife out."

I nodded my head, "yeah, me too" silently received and identified. I stood behind him until the silence got embarrassing.
"Busy?" I asked. He turned round. He was a big guy. In both ways. Tall and leaning towards being big boned – which I am told is the pc way of saying fat – but friendly enough.
As always, impeccably turned in a sharp grey suit, snow white shirt and a tie that indicated Old School or something similar.

What some would call overdressed for Aldi's. Some would also say he was just a little bit gay. Homophobic? Me? Naw, I love my house. It just doesn't like me.

"Just a few things then I am off down the allotment." He replied. The line moved up one.

"Oh, I didn't know you had an allotment" I said for something to say rather than because I was interested.

He puffed up his already puffed up chest. "Oh, yes" he said with a note of pride in his voice. "Had it just over a year now. Best thing I ever did. Fresh vegetables, fresh air, good exercise, people to talk to. And, best of all, it GETS ME OUT OF THE HOUSE"

No, he didn't shout those last six words but he might have well have done. They reverberated around my skull and I clung onto them. Clung on like a drowning man to a thrown life jacket. My heart speeded up. I could feel the acrid taste of adrenaline in my mouth. My thoughts began to trip over themselves.

"Er, any vacancies?" I asked as nonchalantly as I could.

He considered this as we shuffled up one exiting customer more. What was taking the time? "Not at the moment. And there is a waiting list. Why, are you interested?"

"I could be. I seem to have a lot of time on my hands since I retired. Fresh vegetables and exercise sound good." And it will GET ME OUT OF THE HOUSE I didn't say.

In front of us, the middle-aged lady who had just finished with the scanning, price ringing and transferring goods into her trolley suddenly decided to rummage for her purse. We watched as she tipped her bags out, put everything back, checked her pockets and suddenly cheerfully announced "Must have left it in the car. Won't be a moment." She told us as she walked out of the store.

My fellow queuee turned to me. "Why do they leave it until the last moment to get their money out?" he asked. I don't think he expected an answer. "She knows she will have to pay. She knows she will need her purse. Why can't she get it out ready?" He indicated the wallet in his hand. I held up my wife's purse. He looked quickly away.

"So, about the allotment?...."I asked to fill the embarrassed moment.

"Well…as I said, nothing at the moment. But old Albert is struggling with his and could appreciate the help. And there is a way of getting around the waiting list…." He broke off as he suddenly realised that I wasn't the only person listening. A young woman behind me was obviously waiting to hear about "the way of getting round" method of obtaining her own piece of the Good Life.

The not in the least embarrassed lady returned proudly holding up her purse. " It wasn't in the car after all." She beamed at us. " It was in my jumper pocket all the time. Isn't that funny?" Strangely enough, no one else in the queue thought so.

After shooting off a few invisible arrows at her, my new best "I know how to get an allotment" friend nodded in the direction of the lady behind me. He then gave that peculiar little head nod that men can, and women can't, understand. The secret "I'll tell you about it outside" nod. I returned his nod with the required one eyebrow raised "ok" reply.
Finally, after enquiring about the till lady's husband, children, evening meal and the latest soap development, the middle-aged lady grudgingly surrendered her position and, to a silent cheer, pushed her trolley out of the store. Two in front and then my turn. I am beginning to see why I have been allowed to go shopping on my own.

Because the two in front of me were men, it was quickly my turn. Like most men, I had organised my shopping on the conveyor. Heavy stuff first, then lighter and, finally, bread, eggs and the like last. Heavy items into the trolley first and then the rest. Nothing broken, no drama, no fuss..

Outside, I quickly spotted my fellow queuee. He was transferring into a late model BMW 7 Series that was three cars down from Lynne's little Daihatsu. Lynne's little 14 year old Daihatsu estate.

I suddenly wished I had used my almost new Toyota Landcruiser. But, I didn't want any supermarket trolley dings in that.

My new best friend gave a little condescending nod in my general direction. "They don't make them like that any more." He remarked. "Just as well because they were bloody rubbish when they did" was the implied but silent assessment.

I gritted my teeth. It wouldn't do to upset my new best friend. At least not until I had prised his secrets from him. I finished unloading and returned my trolley. I took his as well. A little brown nosing wouldn't hurt, I reasoned.

I gave him back his trolley token and held out my hand.

"Anyway, I'm Dave." I offered. He looked at my hand carefully then, with an "If I must" reluctance, shook mine.

"Geoffrey" he grudgingly replied.

"About this allotment......" I began. Already his eyes were beginning to glaze over. Obviously regretting that moment of pride and one upmanship that had allowed his allotment status to slip out.

"I have to get back." He told me. "I didn't realise how late it was. That stupid woman and her purse....."

"Ok, no problem. You said you were going down after shopping? How about I come down with you and you can show me your allotment. I'll bet it is one of the best down there?" Sometimes I have no shame.

I could almost see the thought process. "Take this owner of an ancient car down to the allotment?" competing with "He'll be impressed when he sees my allotment."
Sometimes you get lucky in life. This was one of those times. "Call for me at two and we can walk down together. You know where I live?" This last ditch hope cruelly dashed as I nodded my head. "Number 196. You can't miss it. One of the nicest houses in the road" I was really into BS mode now. "I'll see you at two, Geoff."
A pained look crossed his face as he got into his car. "Actually, it's Geoffrey."

"Oh sorry, Geoffrey, I won't forget. I prefer to be called by my full name, David, as well. It's terrible how people just shorten things isn't it? See you at two, Geoffrey. "

I waved him all the way out of the car park. I wasn't feeling very proud of myself. I felt dirty, degraded but desperate. I really needed to GET OUT OF THE HOUSE.

Back home, I put everything away and made a cup of tea.

On the road, I used to drink gallons of coffee and countless cigarettes. I gave up smoking, after a mammoth and tortuous effort, five years, four months, two days and five hours ago. Now it doesn't bother me a bit. I rarely get the urge for a quick drag. I don't drink much coffee either. Now it is mainly tea. Straight up without the usual three sugars I enjoyed as a devotee of the dreaded weed.

Lynne came in and I made her a cup of tea as well. She drank it as she put the shopping in its proper place. I told her about meeting Geoff. Sorry, Geoffrey.

"Old Mr Smarmy?" she asked.

" I didn't get his surname." I said. "But, I am going to meet him at two." She gave me a "why the hell are you doing that?" kind of look. Quickly followed up by a "Are you on the turn?" raised eyebrows stare.

" He's got an allotment. " I informed her. *Didn't have that bit of gossip did you? You may have lived here longer than I have but you didn't know that little titbit." I thought smugly.*

"Yes, I know. His wife told me in M&S the other day. She's a bit stuck up but ok most of the time. A bit older than him. The funny thing was that she was buying vegetables. Apparently he keeps bringing stuff home." She laughed. " Skinny mini-carrots, scabby little potatoes and slug eaten cabbages. She has to throw it all away, replace it and let him think it's all his when she serves it up."

I digested this bit of news. "But he said he grows his own vegetables, gets exercise and keeps healthy."

"Rubbish. The allotment is more of a pensioners club. All the wrinkleys go there, sit around in chairs and gossip most of the time. Geoff's wife went down there one day after he had forgotten his flask of Chardonnay and smoked salmon sandwiches."

Lynne took another swig of tea and smiled as she continued. "There were about eight of them sitting in a circle. As soon as they spotted her, they all got up and pretended to be busy. The only reason she doesn't say anything is because it GETS HIM OUT OF THE HOUSE. Why? Are you thinking of getting one?"

"I'm thinking about it"

"What? Don't mumble."

I raised my voice. " I said I am thinking about it. Won't hurt to have a look, will it?"

"Why?"

"Oh, I don't know. Something to do. It'll GET ME OUT OF THE HOUSE, won't it?"

She gave me one of those funny little looks and continued putting the shopping stuff back in its proper place.

2: <u>The Allotment!</u>

We live in Rugby. Famous more notably for the school, the game, the station, Frank Whittle and Rupert Brooke.

Our house is situated in Hillmorton which is one of the older and, perhaps, better areas to live in. Better in that it is less congested, older and more pleasant than the new housing areas that are mushrooming up everywhere on the constantly expanding fringes of the town.

Victory Drive, where we live, is one of those streets that struggle to live up to its name. With a name like that you'd expect a bit of class, wouldn't you? A little Hyacinth Bucketish air of superiority.

Well, first off, it's not exactly a drive. It probably used to be but then it expanded. Now it is one of the main roads into and out of town. Where we live is split into two by a stretch of dual carriageway.

The middle bit is grass with lots of different trees struggling to survive on a minimum of water and maximum of traffic fumes.

It is also on a bit of a slope. One side is higher than the other. Either side has the same assortment of detached and semi detached properties built after the last war. Hence Victory Drive.

The sort of properties that were built to last and not to a price. Substantial houses built with proper respect and craftsmanship. But, for some reason, the owners of the houses on the High Side tend to look down on we Low Siders. Literally and figuratively.

Geoff's house, naturally, was on the High Side. Across from mine but four houses down. Miles, nay continents, apart in imagined status.

Our kitchen window looks out onto the Drive. Because we are not High Siders, we tend to drink our tea and coffee in the kitchen so we see a lot of the activity going on. I finished my drink and looked at the kitchen clock. "Time I was going."
Lynne looked at me. "You're going like that?"
I looked down. Jeans, tee shirt, sensible shoes. Man at Oxfam chic. "Yeah?"
She shrugged and went into the garden.

I walked up the path and had my customary struggle to open the gate. It leans to one side and sticks a bit. But, don't worry, it's on my To Do list. It's been there for about five years now but I'll get around to it. Eventually. If the House lets me.

We Low Siders have made a path across the great central divide. It makes it easy to cross without trudging across mud, dog crap, grass and the endless amount of litter that tends to accumulate. I crossed over from Low to High Society and approached Geoff's house.
The houses either side have, in the main, all dug out their front gardens and brick paved access for their multiple vehicles, mobile homes and campervans.

All except Geoff's. His detached house had box hedge borders and an ice rink smooth tarmac path with parked, almost obligatory, BMW. Later on, after being in full view of envious passers-by, it would be driven into the garage.

The miniscule front lawn had been trimmed to within an inch of its life. A tasteful solar powered Boy and Dolphin statuette complete with flowing water was under the bay window.

An engraved metal sign told me I was at the Leighton-Bradbury residence. I sort of expected an elaborate door pull with bells system but it was just a plain white door bell. Less is More, right?

The door was answered by the Lady of the House. Mrs. Leighton-Bradbury herself. She was a well maintained older woman. Older than her husband old. Immaculate hair, nicely dressed in San Michel's best. Twin set and pearls never really went out of fashion did it?

She was wearing the sort of make up that a lot of short sighted older ladies don't apply very well. A bit hit and miss. More miss.

Her foundation powder was definitely uneven. For some reason this reminded me that pointing my chimney is also on my To Do list. I'll get to it, I promised myself.

She looked at me and her nose wrinkled as if some sort of particularly pungent smell had just wafted underneath it.

"Yes?" she asked raising a pencilled in eyebrow that was noticeably higher than the other one. It gave her face a strange lopsided look.

"Good afternoon. I've come for Geoff."

"Geoffrey" she turned away and spoke into the house. " Someone for you". *A gardener or window cleaner type person* was obviously the unspoken assessment.

I heard footsteps in the hallway and then Geoffrey appeared. "Oh, it's you" he said. He turned to his lady wife. "Darling, this is Dereck, he lives over the road." *On the Lower Side* was definitely implied.

" Dave" I corrected him as I held out my hand to her. She looked at it and then turned around. "Don't be late". were her parting words. "Bye, nice meeting you" I called after her back.

Geoff was dressed for the allotment. Jeans with razor sharp creases, a sort of lumberjack padded shirt and a nicely knotted cravat around his neck. For some reason, the letters YMCA popped into my mind.

In one hand he held a pair of yellow, workmen type, leather gloves. The other was holding a pair of green wellingtons. The posh designer sort with brown seams and little tassels. Deep 4x4 go anywhere treads. He put them on.

"We'd better go then" he said with a sort of Dead Man Walking desperation. "I'll just go on ahead a bit" he told me as he practically sprinted down the drive.

I got the message, nearly told him where to go but needs must, right?.

Five minutes of following him and then he turned into a little side path. I would have called it a ginnel but there was probably a more suitable High Side alternative.

At the back of the High Side houses there is open woodland. People walk their dogs there. Horses get exercised. Some Low Side types just walk and chat to each other.

The ginnel/side path led between two houses into this public place. At the end of the path, on the right, was a pair of substantial metal gates with a chain-link fence attached to either side. A sign on the gates informed me that "These gates must be kept locked at all times".

Geoff put his hand into his pocket and pulled out a keyring. I noticed that it had a BMW fob on it. He put the single key into the heavy duty padlock and opened one of the gates. Waiting for me to pass through, he shut the gate and locked it again.

The path led into a little spinney of worn looking trees. There was a tunnel like effect as we walked down from bright sunlight into its darkness and shade. I could hear a little brook tinkling on one side. No, on closer inspection, it was an open drain.

At the other end we walked into the sun again and everything changed. We were standing in a large open space

There was a main path and on either side fenced off plots of land with sheds of various sizes, condition and ingenuity on each plot.

"The Victory Allotments" Geoff said almost reverently with an all encompassing wave of his hand. "What do you think?"

I ignored the first thought that popped into my head. I looked around. "Er, it looks very nice. How big is the whole allotment? Is each plot the same size?"

"Almost two acres and there are approximately 40 allotments. Some are large plots and some are half plots. A lot of people start off with half plots then, if another adjacent half plot becomes available, they can expand into a large plot" he explained

"The allotments were started during the war in the Dig for Victory campaign and have continued ever since. Originally there were more plots but it has now settled into what you see. If the council can't rent a large plot, it tends to split it into two again so the actual number of plots fluctuates."

I continued to look around as walked down the main path. Lots of other little paths weaved down and around the plots.

The condition of each plot seemed to vary. Some were obviously well tended with clearly defined boundaries and a neat and tidy appearance. Others seemed to have reverted back to the wild with just a few forlorn looking canes stuck in a corner or a little patch of dug earth.

"I was expecting something else." I said as we walked. "The ones I see on the telly are all large with lots of cheerful people smiling as they work. They seem to grow some impressive vegetables as well."

"Yes, well that's tv for you." Geoff said in an exasperated tone. Was it my imagination or was he actually becoming more human once away from his house? "Every time there is a new gardening programme , the council get inundated with allotment requests.

The new people come and find out that it is not quite so easy. It is hard work and it takes time. On the tv, stuff is planted and the next week is fully grown and harvested. In reality, it is different." he expanded.

"People start with good intentions but lose enthusiasm when the weather and pests ruin their crops. Mainly they find it much harder work than depicted on the telly. Usually they just pack up and go after a few weeks." We continued walking.

"The plot then lies empty until the next gardening programme and then the cycle starts again. There are about 20 die hard people here. Some have been here since it began. Old Albert is one of those."

He stopped in front of a plot on the right. "Well, here it is." He said proudly with a 'welcome to my kingdom' all encompassing wave. "what do you think?"

In front of me was an obviously new chain link fence. It continued up the sides of the plot to the top where it was met by the boundary hedge.

Inside the fence was a paved area with an equally new shed standing proudly. And, not just any old shed.

This was large, about 12 foot by 8, with a covered exterior veranda area. More of a extended summer house than shed.

I looked around at the neighboring sheds. Many were old and had seem much better days.

New pieces of wood and felt showed recent or on-going renovation. Most seemed afterthoughts along the lines of "I know, I have all this wood, why don't I make a shed?" construction. In contrast Geoff's building seemed to dwarf and sneer at its companions.

"Very nice" was what I felt was the expected response. "Such a difference to the others. Your whole plot seems so much better." I laid it on with a large trowel. Remember I still wanted to get down here, right?

"Yes" he almost smirked. "Some of them are in a right state. Most get old sheds from somewhere else and just plonk them down. Some even build their own. I prefer to do things differently.

That is why I have raised beds rather than just an open plot. The people on the tv seem to think raised beds are better and I agree. So much easier to manage." Again he used the regal wave as he indicated his.

I counted. He had six raised beds. They were basically two tiers of scaffolding planks along the sides with half planks at the end. Scaffolding poles were driven into the earth at each corner to act as supports. The interiors were filled to the top with earth.

They were laid lengthways up the allotment with three on either side. There were a variety of vegetables struggling gamely to survive in each raised bed. The spaces between the beds were all neatly paved.

An open area at the top end had potatoes growing in neat ridges.

I had to admit I was impressed. The difference between this plot and the others couldn't be more marked. Obviously a lot of hard graft had gone into it. Had I underestimated my new best friend?

"Golly Geoffrey, this is most impressive. You have really gone to town haven't you? Must have taken you ages. And, such a lot of work. You must be really proud?"

He preened at my praise then his face fell. He seemed to be thinking and then clearly arrived at a decision.

"Um, I didn't actually do all this. I don't really have the time. I had some men come in and sort out the beds, the shed and the paving. I did supervise though so that is really the same thing, isn't it?"

No, it isn't, Geoff. "Of course" I said
brightly. "Got to have any project
managed properly. Christopher Wren
didn't actually build St Paul's did he?
But everyone always associates the
cathedral with him, don't they? I think
you have done a marvelous job." *I'm
getting really good at this BS, aren't I?*

Whilst digesting this incredible piece
of information, I had another thought.
I looked around and realised what had
been niggling me. "Where are the
people?" I asked. "I can't see anyone. I
had a vision of people toiling away
and lots of cheerful banter."
"Well, it is a bit late. Most people come
in the morning or evening before or
after work. Some of the retired
regulars stop till around mid-day then
go home. It varies".

"Oh, I see." Then I had another
thought. "So, what are you going to do
now? And, when am I going to see
Albert?"

In answer, he produced another key from his pocket and opened an industrial size padlock on the shed door. "First of all, I am going to have a drink of tea. Would you like one?"

Without waiting for an answer he entered his shed/summer house/status symbol. He emerged again with a couple of plastic chairs. Plonking them down on the veranda, he went back in and carried out a white plastic table. Setting them up, he indicated that I should sit.

I sat. It was actually quite pleasant. The sun was shining, birds whistled as they hopped up and down looking for food. I could see and hear the wind moving the boundary trees. I could get used to this.

In the far background I could see a raised mound. I was just trying to work out what it was when there was a rumbling, clattering noise and a train sped past. Of course, the railway. The West Coast Mainline. Coming up from Euston to Rugby, Birmingham, Crewe and beyond.

Sometimes, when the wind was in the right direction, I could hear the trains at home. I hadn't realised our house was so close. I also had the thought that I must have passed these allotments many times on my frequent journalistic train journeys to London.

"How do you take it?" I looked inside and saw Geoff putting a kettle onto a gas ring. Intrigued, I went inside.

Inside there was a wide shelf/table area down one side. Underneath, a row of drawers from which he was taking two cups. There was a substantial metal locker in one corner. There was carpet on the floor and even a door mat. A print of Turner's The Haywain graced the far wall. Interestingly, a single bed with pillow and blanket was underneath it.

A row of tools were clipped into place on one wall. They didn't look as if they had seen much use. Whilst the water was boiling, he opened the metal locker with yet another key. Inside was a radio and a battery powered tv. He took the tv out and placed it on the table area. "Works off that car battery in the locker." He explained. "Which is recharged by a solar panel in the roof. I sometimes watch the racing." He added defensively.

"Might as well be comfortable." I agreed. "No need to rough it. I have to admit, you have got it kitted out very nicely indeed."

He nodded and then, with a rush...."Er, no need to broadcast it. The wife doesn't know what sort of set-up I have down here. She thinks it is just a plot of land and a little shed. She doesn't have to know, does she?" *Not if it gets me my allotment, she doesn't.* "No, of course not, Geoffrey. Nothing to do with me." I reassured him.

"Um.....it's just that I like to be on my own sometimes. I find it quite restful here. Watch a bit of tv, have a drink, bit of a nap in the afternoon." He admitted. *Deeper and deeper into my debt. It's in the bag.*

"Can't leave much time for growing stuff." I observed. He looked at me. Weighed me up and then, with an in for a penny, in for a pound desperation blurted out...."Actually, our house gardener comes down and helps out here as well."

3: <u>The Allotment!</u>

Albert "Bert" Collins shut his front door firmly and walked to his van. He was going, as he did twice daily, to his allotment.

Walk was perhaps a simplistic way to describe the way he moved. It wasn't so much a walk as a rolling gait. The way big boned people moved. But, seen from the front at least, Collins wasn't fat. If anything he gave the appearance of being slim.

He was around average height, in his mid-thirties with a weather beaten face. Looking similar to Jack Nicholson on a bad face day with an order of extra wrinkles on the side. The sort of face you liked or didn't.

The hair he had left was firmly brushed forward from the back and over his forehead into a Roman style fringe. A forehead tan line showed that he normally wore some sort of headgear.

He was wearing tan, mid thigh, safety boots, jeans and a brown shirt. A large brown belt around his waist was supplemented by a pair of wide red braces. If nothing else, he could truthfully be called a belt and braces type of person.

It was when seen from the side that the reason for his peculiar gait was obvious. His side profile showed a large extended belly. It could be best likened to the side view that very pregnant ladies present. Obviously he wasn't pregnant but he had the same straight back and waddle.

His face didn't have the broken veined appearance of a heavy drinker. But, whether from drink, some glandular problem or something more serious, it was an extra burden to carry around. Fortunately, the forward weight was compensated for by the large chip on his shoulder.

The bad attitude he carried around was in-bred. His father had it as well. Most people are born happy then develop their fears, phobias and attitudes as they develop. A few babies are delivered screaming hatred at the world. Collins was one of these.

He developed from the schoolboy that nobody befriended, picked for a team or just ignored, to the teenager who was always in trouble for bullying or outright intimidation. Not with just the law but everyone. No-one had a good word to say for him or about him.

He had never married. Picking up girls was never the problem He could switch on the charm when required and many women were attracted to his bad boy looks and reputation.

Maintaining a relationship was the problem. He couldn't keep the Mr Nice Guy persona going for long and inevitably reverted to his true self. His usual way of solving an argument or debate was to lash out. And, also inevitably, that lead to the end of yet another relationship.

The last time a woman had lived in his house was three years ago.

Each failed attempt just added yet another layer to the hate and hostility that, along with his protruding stomach, he nurtured and carried with him.

He lived in Dunchurch, an ever developing village on the outskirts of Rugby. Dunchurch was once an important staging post on the coaching road between London and Holyhead. Its other claim to fame is the house where Guy Fawkes is said to have hatched the Gunpowder Plot.

Another Dunchurch landmark is the statue of Lord John Scott, an 18th century landlord and Scottish mp. This stands in the village and, for the last 30 years around Christmas time, is dressed in a variety of costumes by local pranksters.

Bert Collins had never been invited to be one of these pranksters. He lived in the same council house he had been born into.

His parents were dead. His mother from overwork and abuse. His father from drink. When his father died, the tenancy, of the house passed to him.

He wasn't really interested in the statue, the village or anything in Dunchurch. Not since the Allotment Incident.

The allotments in Dunchurch were situated alongside the busy A 45 trunk road. Like most allotments it had been started during WW2 and had continued ever since. It differed to many allotments in that is was privately and not council run.

The Dunchurch Road Allotment Committee was comprised of allotment holders. It set the annual fee, decided who joined and how it was run.

Collins had taken over the allotment in the same way as he had his house. When his father had died he had just turned up and declared his intention to carry on.

Unfortunately this didn't sit well with the Allotment Committee who, after having put up with his father, weren't that keen to have another Collins trying to run the allotment his way.

However, it was decided to give him a chance and he was offered a probationary tenancy. It was a decision that the Committee very soon regretted.

The Collins allotment was well maintained, productive and an outstanding example of what an allotment plot should be. The problem was the attitude of the previous and the now current tenant.

Neither of the Collins liked being told what to do. To them, rules and regulations were for other people. Collins senior had always seemed to be at loggerheads with the Committee. Collins junior continued with the family tradition.

The other tenants, on Committee instructions, all painted their sheds Forest Green to give a uniformity to the appearance of the Dunchurch Road allotments. The bright red shed on the Collins plot screamed both insult and visual injury.

When water rationing was introduced, every other tenant adhered to the request to save water. Colllins was caught using sprinklers, kept on overnight, on his potatoes.

He continuously tried to overturn the Committee's authority with inevitable results. He was asked to leave. He refused and arrived one morning to find his shed dismantled and , along with his tools, on the other side of the allotment gates. Gates that now had a brand new heavy duty padlock.

He complained and fumed but couldn't alter the decision.

He tried in vain to find another allotment. Eventually he heard of a vacant plot on the Victory Allotments in Hillmorton. A bit of a journey but, more importantly, council owned and operated.

Which meant very little interference and, given that he knew someone in the Council's Parks and Recreation office, he knew he would get the vacancy.

Also that there was very little likelihood of being turfed off for some mindless rule or regulation breach.

The fact that he held a very juicy bit of scandalous information over his contact's head, practically guaranteed that.

During the last five years Collins had expanded into two large plots and, to all intents and purposes, was in unofficial charge of the lower half of the Victory allotments.

4: <u>The Allotment!</u>

It was pleasant just sitting there. A warm May morning. A cup of Darjeeling, feet up on the veranda, just chilling. I could get used to this. Which reminded me.

"Uh…Geoffrey, when can I get to meet this Albert? Is his plot near this one? What's the situation about getting past the waiting list and getting my own allotment?"

He took his time. Obviously either regretting what he said in the supermarket or just talk? I waited.

"First off, there is a way of getting past the waiting list. Although, with so many empty plots just now, I can't think why the council should insist there is a waiting list at all." He queried. " You just have to get an existing plot tenant to take you on as his co-worker."

"That's it?" I asked. " Doesn't seem too hard. Where does Albert come into it?"

"Albert has the plot at the end on the right. Plot number 1. He's had it since the allotments opened and was the very first tenant. He's pushing ninety now and just potters.

He can't do the heavy work so is looking for a helper. Basically, he informs the council that he is getting a co-worker. The council usually agree and you would become his official helper. On what basis, you would have to work out with Albert." He explained.

"Several of the older guys have helpers and it is usually on a 50-50 basis. You do all the heavy work and split the produce equally. If the tenant gives up his plot, for whatever reason, his co-worker is given first option of taking it over. That's the loophole for jumping the waiting list."

"Hm.. sounds simple. Is that what you did?" I asked.

" No." he replied most indignantly. "I was on the waiting list for quite a long time. Eventually, I was offered this one. It was a bit run down but I managed to get it into shape."

No Geoff, your gardener and several beefy blokes did. "I can see you have worked really hard. This must be the best plot down here." I trowelled the BS smoothly. "So Albert is willing, is he?"

"The last time we talked he mentioned it. He lives in the house on the end and has a gate from his garden to the plot. You would have to go round and ask him. Tell him I sent you." He added graciously.

"It sounds just what I need. Since I retired, I seem to have too much time on my hands. This would be great. Not that I could have a set up like yours" I added quickly.

"Well, it takes time. What line were you in?" not really interested but pretending to be.

"When I sold my international haulage operation I moved into media communications." I said thinking quickly. A one truck haulier and a free lance writer wouldn't have overly impressed him. Besides, it was true.

The effect was almost instant. You could see it on his face. Maybe he had underestimated this oaf? "Gosh, I didn't know" he confessed. "That must have been interesting?"

Before I could reply he carried on telling me about himself. His years in banking and how his present deputy manager position would soon change into being promoted to manage his own High Street branch.

How he was currently on holiday and usually only managed week-ends and the occasional half day down here.

"You sound like a very busy man." I managed to get in edgeways. "Obviously why you need help yourself. Maybe I could be your co-worker? " I offered as if the thought had just struck me. *Besides which, I know all your secrets now Geoff.*

I loved seeing the look of alarm cross his face. He back pedalled furiously. " I really think that Albert's plot would suit you better. You look as if you like doing things your own way. Getting Albert's plot would enable you to mould his run-down patch into your own ideal plot, wouldn't it?"

I suddenly had this revelation. I blurted it out without thinking. "You have another reason for being down here, don't you?"

He went white and I knew instantly that I was right. "You sly old dog. You've got someone on the side, haven't you?"

He nodded shamefully. "Yes" he said in a whisper. He looked up . " You won't tell anyone, will you?" he pleaded.

" Of course I won't Geoffrey. None of my business. Besides which, we are friends now aren't we?" I held out my hand to seal our pact.

He chose the lesser of the two evils. Grudgingly he took my hand. "Thank you".

He then went on to explain how he had started his affair almost three years ago. How, with both being married, their meetings were getting more and more difficult. How the allotment had come up and the possibilities it offered. Hence also the luxurious "shed", the bed and the other trappings. "We have spent some wonderful times down here."

"But, what about the other people down here? Surely they must know?"

"Not really. Oh, some must have their suspicions but nobody says anything. I am a bit older than my friend." He explained sheepishly.

"To my knowledge only one person down here knows for sure. And that is only because he caught us in bed together one afternoon. But he won't tell either."

Just at that moment, we both heard a loud metallic sound. I swiveled my head around but couldn't place it.

"It's the front gate." Geoff explained that we had come through the 'back' gate. The front entrance gate was at the end of the path on the right.

This entrance was off the main road. There was a car park and most of the tenants used it. Only the locals walked and saved a journey by using the gate we had used.

Now I had the direction, I could indeed see a gate being opened. Someone entered, shut the gate behind them, and started to walk in our direction.

As the figure got nearer I could see it was a man. He was wearing tan boots, jeans and a brown shirt. Bright red braces and a red baseball cap. He had a curious rolling gait.

"Oh dear." Geoff whispered urgently. "That's Bert Collins. Just leave this to me. Don't say anything to upset him. He's a bit volatile." He was almost pleading now.

The man stopped on the path besides us. He had an unpleasant looking face with little piggy eyes and almost lipless mouth. The kind of face that turned milk into yogurt just by looking at it.

He looked at Geoff angrily. "Where is it then, you fat bastard?" he spat out.

"...Sorry Bert, I just need an extra day or so. I'll get it , I promise."

"Not good enough. We had a deal." He suddenly reached out across the fence and grabbed Geoff by his cravat. He started to pull him towards the fence.

Geoff stumbled forward and then fell as he reached the fence. He ended up folded over it struggling for breath as his neckwear got pulled even tighter. The newcomer jerked his head up to eye level. He stared into his Geoff's eyes. "Don't cross me you little nonce."

Right about this time, I reached over and grabbed the arm that was tightening my new friend's silk cravat.

I am only average height but very strong for my stature and age. Years of truck driving, loading and unloading and just a natural strength had toned me.

Anyone looking at me wouldn't have been very impressed. I'm around five eight, still fairly slim and must look like a lot of other guys my age . More of an eight pack than a six. Old, decrepit and harmless.

So, when I grabbed his arm and squeezed it must have been a shock. Even more so when he felt the pressure I was using. I increased that pressure.

He tried to swat my hand away with his other hand. I squeezed even harder and was rewarded with a gasp of pain. Using my free hand, I unlatched the grasp he had on Geoff and dragged him towards me.

We were eyeball to eyeball over the fence. Suddenly his free arm came towards my head in what was intended to be a knock out punch. Instinctively I grabbed his fist and, with an effort, halted it in mid swing. By now I was good and angry and my temper, which I normally keep under control, was up

Keeping my eyes locked on his, I started to squeeze with both hands. One on his arm and the other around his closed fist. He struggled wildly but I just increased the pressure.

His expression changed from aggression to bewilderment and then to fear. Suddenly all the fight went out of him. The tension went from his body and he sagged. I used the opportunity to bring him slowly to his knees.

You could see he didn't like it but he had no choice. Relentlessly I pushed him down using his arms as leverage. When he was kneeling before me, I released my grip and pushed him backwards.

Whilst he was falling I quickly got over the fence and stood beside him. He lay there with confusion in his eyes. I guessed this was not the way things normally worked out for him. I gave him a good kick in the ribs to make up for the punch he had tried to land.

I believed in always kicking someone when they are down. Put them down, keep them down, had always worked for me.

"Had enough?" I asked. He didn't say anything so I kicked him again. I only had sensible shoes on so couldn't land as hard a kick as I really wanted to.

I am not normally a violent person but bullies always get me riled up. I had suffered more than enough at school from bullies.

On the road, I had met many men like the one lying at my feet. Men who liked to get what they wanted by violence and fear. And, I had learnt one positive lesson.

Most bullies are cowards. They are not used to people standing up to them. When they meet someone who is their equal or more they always back down. Just like this specimen who couldn't meet my eyes.

"I'm going to keep kicking you until you tell me to stop." I informed him. I drew back my foot..." have you had enough yet?"

He nodded his head vigorously. Not good enough.

"Say it." I said in a loud voice.

All the fight went out of him. "I've had enough, I've had enough. No more."

"Get up" I commanded.

He rose slowly , unable to meet my eyes. "What's your name?" I said in a voice still tight with anger and adrenaline.

"Bert Collins" he said in a very low voice.

I turned to Geoff. "What the hell is all this about?"

" I owe him some money." He admitted nervously.

"Must be a fair bit for him to act like that. What's it for?"

Geoff looked at Collins then at me. He came to some sort of decision. "He found out about my affair. He wanted money to keep quiet." He admitted quietly.

Collins was glaring at him trying to intimidate him. I gave him another kick. " He was blackmailing you?"

Geoff nodded. "£50 a week."

"How long for? How much?"

"Eight weeks. £400. I couldn't get it this week because of unexpected bills. He wanted it yesterday. I told him I would have it today. I didn't expect you to be here."

I looked down at Collins. "So, not only a bully. A blackmailer as well" I looked over. "Do you want it back. Call the police?"

He shook his head vigorously. No, that's all right. I don't want to take it any further" he said. "Lets just drop the matter."

"You happy with that?" I spat out at the prone figure on the path. I hate men like him. People who prey on the weak and try to profit from them

" The idiot deserved it" he tried to explain. "He can afford it."

"You just listen. " I gave him another tap on his ribs. "If I want any of that crap out of you, I'll just squeeze your head. All right?"

He nodded his head. I told him to get up. Her did so with difficulty holding his ribs.

"Well then, Bert Collins, I suggest that you clear off out of here and don't bother my friend again. IS THAT CLEAR?"

"Yes" he said pathetically quickly. He half walked, half stumbled off back towards the main gate.

I turned round to Geoff. He was looking at me with his mouth open. Suddenly he doubled over and was violently sick over the path. I waited until he had finished, took him back onto the veranda and sat him down.

"You feeling better now." I asked in a more normal voice. He looked at me fearfully. Like I was some sort of monster. "That....that was Bert Collins." He gasped.

"Yeah, so he said. But, don't worry, he won't bother you again. Not while I'm down here. Now...."I rubbed my hands together briskly...."how do we get hold of old Albert?"

He was still looking at me as if I had two heads. His mouth was working but no sound came out. His eyes kept darting from me to the shuffling figure of the departing Collins. He swallowed and tried to get some saliva into his dry mouth.

After a few false starts he suddenly blurted out "Uh..... how about if you became my co-worker instead?" he asked in a croaky voice and with wide, still disbelieving, eyes.

Oh yes, I've still got it. Result! "Well." I said as I considered it. A set up like this? "Well... if you are sure Geoff."

"Oh yes" he said in an increasingly firmer voice. Someone who Collins is afraid of? "Oh yes, I am very sure."

5: The Allotment!

Everything happened pretty quickly after that. Geoff informed the council that he had a co-worker and that was pretty much that. A chance encounter in Aldi's and, a week later, I was officially a co-worker.

Lynne was surprised when I told her the news. Sort of glad too. She made a big thing of sending me off with a little lunch box and a flask. I hadn't told her what Geoff's set-up was like. It might have got too complicated.

Oh, and by the way, I met Geoff's gardener after I officially started. I saw someone in our plot as I wandered down the path. Not knowing what was going on, I hurried up and got a better look. After the Collins incident, I had been fearing some sort of revenge attack.

"Can I help you?" I shouted up the path.

The intruder turned round. "No, you're all right. I'm just checking the cabbages for slugs. I'm Geoff's gardener."

That was when I got a better look. She was mid-twenties, slim, good looking. Everything you could want in a gardener.

My brain cells might be slowing down but they still worked. Not only a gardener but Geoff's whole reason for being down here in the first place.

I shook hands with Geoff's special friend.

Actually she was very nice. Jane was her name but she was definitely not plain. I could see what my co-shirker saw in her.

Geoff must have told her that I knew the score because shortly afterwards there was no more pretence at doing any "gardening". I became solely in charge of the upkeep for Plot number 9.

Geoff and Jane were never in any danger of getting sunburnt. At least not down the allotment. They spent most of their time locked away in the shed.

Of course, everyone on this section of the top allotments knew what was going on. I reckon they guessed that the subdued screaming and moaning from the shed wasn't coming from the soundtrack of a porn dvd. Nothing was ever said.

I said the top allotments because the allotments, like Victory Drive, had a higher and lower sub division. Top and Bottom as they were referred to. I found myself in the unaccustomed position of being in the Top section. Even allotments have their class system.

The Bottom section was two rows of plots almost directly opposite the main entrance. The farthest plots were almost always empty because they were so wet and boggy.

I had been at the allotments for almost three months by now. During that time I had seen a constant stream of "newbies" come and go down the Bottom section.

They would arrive full of enthusiasm with brand new tools and big plans. Dads, mums and kids dreaming the dream. Living the Good Life. A few weeks of hard digging, planting and very little success in terms of produce, quickly drained the enthusiasm. The almost daily appearance became limited to week-ends.

Then there would be no appearance for a couple of weeks. As the plot gradually deteriorated, it was finally accepted that yet another tenant had left. And so the cycle would begin again.

Very few stayed the course. Those that did eventually began to reap the rewards of their labours. And, more importantly, became accepted amongst the hard core plot holders.

After three months of almost daily appearances, weeding, digging and planting I was at the head nodding stage with my immediate neighbours.

Truck driving is a lonely occupation so I was used to being on my own. I tend to treat people as they treat me. If they are polite so am I. If they want a chat, and I have the time, then I will chat. They want a hand or a little help then I'm your man. If they prefer to be left alone then I leave them alone.

I had long ago given up trying to deliberately impress people. People accept you or they don't. What they say to your face is usually totally different to what they say behind your back. So still being treated as a Newbie didn't bother me.

Geoff was still a Newbie after nearly a year. But, it bothered him that people were stand-offish. In his position he was used to a certain respect. Staff were deferential to him. Customers sought his advice and help. He really couldn't understand the total indifference he got on the allotment site.

When we had a tea break –on the rare occasions he turned up whilst I was still there – he used to anguish about it. He just couldn't understand the concept of earning respect or slowly building up friendships.

He also didn't realise that his manner, dress sense and implied superiority tended to put people off. Banging an attractive lady friend didn't help his cause either. People tend to get jealous.

But, if nothing else, the unwritten and undeclared concept of "What happens on the allotment stays on the allotment" was firmly upheld on the Victory Allotments.

The only thing Lynne knew for certain about the allotment was that I had become leaner, browner and OUT OF THE HOUSE for most of the morning.

She even kept up the pretence that the vegetables that I proudly dumped on the kitchen worktop were grown and harvested by my own hands, hard labour and green fingers

Great cabbages, long succulent carrots, good potatoes, green beans, eye watering onions, tasty tomatoes and satisfying corn cobs were regular offerings.

She really appreciated that she never had to prepare, wash, de-slug or top and tail any of my produce. And, if she occasionally had to covertly remove a price sticker, she never said anything.

The sad fact was that I had to virtually start again from scratch on Geoff's plot. He and Jane had been too "busy" to really start any plants. What seeds did germinate usually died from lack of care, water or insects and grubs. Even the potatoes were nothing more than marbles due to lack of water, winter manuring or spring fertilizing.

I am not green fingered or anything. Not even a competent gardener. Neat and tidy is my gardening rule. Get rid of the weeds – and usually most of Lynne's new bulbs – mow the lawns regularly and trim the hedges.

But, I did grow up on a farm and understood manuring, watering and crop rotation. I just had to scale down from a 200 hundred acre farm to a council sized allotment plot.

So, gradually I was getting the plot into shape. Planting stuff that could be planted in August –not much – trying to salvage what the love birds had started, digging the raised beds and forking in a load of best manure delivered from a local farm.

But, most of all – and totally unexpectedly – I found I was enjoying it. I had always worked hard and coming into retirement with virtually a full stop had been unsettling. I needed this distraction and the work of the allotment to start to enjoy life again.

Even The House was responding better to my administrations. It had stopped, mostly, sabotaging my work and we had reached a sort of understanding. Even the dreaded To Do list seemed to be getting smaller. Naw, it wasn't really getting smaller but it wasn't getting any bigger either.

Small steps. Slow but sure. Take your time and do it right. Measure twice and cut once. All useless pieces of advice. But, I was getting there and, more importantly, had a reason for getting out of bed each morning.

I was even beginning to enjoy the company of my other allotmenteers. They were talking to me more and more. Giving me advice. Giving me the low down on the allotments, who was regular , who wasn't.

Plot 8 put me in touch with the local allotment association where I could buy seeds, fertilizers and other supplies at reduced prices.

Gradually names were exchanged, "Good Mornings" evolved into longer and more constructive chats. I began to feel a sense of camaraderie and friendship with my fellow allotmenteers.

Around the sixth month, I realised that I had been accepted. All was well with my allotment world. All except for one thing. Or rather one person: Bert Collins.

6: The Allotment!

The Collins empire consisted of two large plots. They were opposite the main gates and, give the guy his due, in excellent shape. This was understandable given that he spent most of his time on his plots.

No one really knew what he did for a living. Some one said he was a self employed carpenter. Another that he was a mobile mechanic. Most guessed he was long term unemployed. No one really knew what he did to get money to live on. I knew that blackmail was one of his options.

One of the guys had a relative who had a plot on the Dunchurch Road allotment. Collins was not so fondly remembered there. So at least everyone knew what to expect and, generally, weren't disappointed.

With no real reason to come up to the Top section, he concentrated on his end. Not only working his plots but working on the other tenants as well. For all his faults, he could turn on the charm when he wanted to. He made a point of befriending every newcomer, giving advice and creating a good first impression.

But, let any one cross him and his real persona was revealed. Anyone working his plot could hear Collins when he started shouting and swearing at the unfortunate he deemed to have crossed him.

Usually it was some one who didn't agree with his advice. Collins didn't want any run down tenanted plots. If people were working the plots then he had a standard he expected to be adhered to.

If the allotments weren't kept in good shape then the council could lose interest in them as well.

There were already rumours that new houses were earmarked for this particular allotment. That was the last thing he wanted.

Plots had to be tidy, weed free, in good order with any shed in good repair. If a quiet "word" didn't work, more progressive methods were used. Weed killer sprayed all over the growing vegetables.

If that didn't work, Collins went to town. Sheds broken into and tools ruined or taken. Water hoses punctured, barrow wheels slashed. Even the victims car tyres were "accidentally" punctured. The pressure mounted to breaking point. The offender either gave in or gave up. Another reason why there were so many empty plots on the lower end.

There was also the "maintenance money" that he tried to extract from the more vulnerable or gullible of them. The latter supposedly to pay for the maintenance of the paths, the borders and any repairs. The council knew nothing of this. In reality, anything collected straight into his back pocket.

And, he was pretty bulletproof. Complain to the council and you complained to his contact in the Parks and Open Spaces department who would file it as vandalism. Complain too loudly and you arrived one morning to find your shed a heap of ashes. This had happened once since I had been there.

Most of those who wouldn't do as he asked just called it a day, cut their losses and left. Those that remained down the Lower end either put up with it or agreed with him.

Essentially the Victory Allotment was split into two camps. The Lower end run by Collins and the Top end occupied by those he couldn't intimidate or co-erce.

But both sides agreed that Collins wouldn't stop until he was in full control. Everyone knew that his ultimate aim was to set up a Committee to run the allotments. And that there could only be one leader of that committee.

I was surprised when it became public knowledge about my run-in with him.

I turned up a couple of days after the incident and my Plot Eight neighbour was already there hoeing weeds. We exchanged "Good Mornings" and then he asked what had happened between Collins and myself.

He was one of those whose back garden had a gate that opened directly into the allotment. He had witnessed the whole incident from his kitchen window. Apparently there had been much speculation amongst the others as to its cause. But even more surprise as to its outcome.

I just told him that there had been words and that Collins had swung a punch. That I had retaliated and that was it. He knew there was more to it – having witnessed the whole thing – but left it at that.

I was later told, when I was finally accepted into their little community, that every one had been waiting to see what happened next. Collins didn't usually take a defeat like that lying down. When nothing did happen, they slowly began to realise that Collins wasn't going to take it any further.

I was warned thought that he hadn't liked being bested and humiliated. Even less when he knew that everyone knew about it. The general consensus was that there would eventually be a payback and I should watch my back.

I was told that Collins liked to go around inspecting everyone's plot. Usually in the evenings when nobody was about. He either forgot that he was in full view from the adjoining houses or didn't care.

I only saw him when I went down to the tap by the front gate. I would look around whilst waiting for my watering can to fill. If he was on his plot next to the tap he would pretend not to notice me.

On the other side of the gate was the car park and opposite that the dilapidated Scout hut where the local pack met weekly. A large sign on the car park side of the gates warned that there were "SECURITY CAMERAS IN OPERATION". It was all a bluff.

There were no cameras and not a lot of other security either. The gates could be easily scaled. The chain-link fencing that surrounded the allotment had been cut or had collapsed in places. Coincidentally these breaks in the fence had only happened in the less visible places.

In short, the allotments were often referred to locally as an open air vegetable supermarket. People just came and helped themselves to whatever was in season or left lying around. But there was little actual vandalism.

Apart from the type of "vandalism" carried out by Collins. And that mainly was restricted to the Lower end.

Our Top end had too many plot holders whose plots were an extension of their back gardens. Any stranger was usually quickly spotted, challenged or half heartedly chased. Until now.

One morning I arrived to find a strong smell of wood smoke on the air. A group of the guys were congregated at the far end of the path.

This plot I knew was old Albert's –the plot I had hoped to co-work until Geoff changed his mind – and the general mood was that of anger.

I looked up the path dividing Plot 1 and Plot 2. Albert's plot wasn't the best maintained. There were a lot weeds and very little else. He wasn't bothered about growing much other than potatoes and raspberries.

These were at the top end. The potatoes next to his back garden gate and the raspberry bushes, strung out on wires supported by metal poles, before or after depending on which gate was used.

Potatoes don't require much work after the initial ground preparation and planting. A bit of watering and a little weeding, digging up, storing and eating.

It was the raspberry crop that was Albert's main interest. He spent a lot of time preparing, planting and cultivating them. He then made them into a very potent raspberry wine, Geoff had told me.

Now they were just a few charred stems sticking forlornly through the wires that had once supported them.

The smell of the ruined crop was slightly nauseating. A mix of burnt wood and the sickly aroma of roasted raspberries. And, as I suddenly detected as I kicked at a still smoldering clump, a definite lingering smell of petrol.

"Some bastard torched them." Said Plot 3. A tall stout guy with a ruddy complexion and swept back white hair. I thought his name was Pete.

"Yeah and it doesn't take much working out who, does it?" said Paul from Plot 15.

"Come on Paul, you don't know for sure. It could have been vandals. " said a little guy whose name I didn't know. His plot was a bit further down from mine on the other side.

"Bit of a coincidence isn't it Mick?" Fred, Plot 10, said to my near neighbour. " Old Albert gets warned by Collins to tidy his plot up or else. This definitely looks like a case of 'or else' to me."

Most of the heads nodded agreement. "Bert Collins!" one spat out. "Bastard." Some of them looked around quickly, almost fearfully. "Still, we don't know for sure, do we?" little Mick persisted. The others turned towards him.

"What is it with you? " said a beefy young guy. " He a friend of yours? You always seem to be defending him."

Mick held up his hands almost as if he was being attacked. "I'm just saying you can't go around accusing people without proof."

"It's bad enough what goes on down on the Lower without it spreading. I say it's time we did something about it once and for all."

The beefy guy turned to me. "What do you think. The word is that you had him on the ground and was kicking seven shades of shit out of him?"

All eyes turned to me. " He was having a go at Geoff. It got a bit heated and I stepped in. Then he swung a punch at me. I defended myself and he ended up on the ground. That's about it." I explained.

"No, it isn't." said Adrian from Plot 8. I saw it all from my window.

"Bert had Geoff over the fence. Dave here grabbed Bert's arm and then his fist when he tried to throw a punch. Next thing, Bert's sinking to his knees. Dave gives him a push and then he's flat on his back. Dave is over the fence and kicking him as he lays there.

After a while, and a few more kicks, Bert gets up and shuffles up the path. Doubled over and holding his ribs. I've never seen anything like it. Bert Collins bested by that guy."

Adrian waves a dismissive hand in my direction. Almost as if to say "Look at him. How did that happen?"

I draw myself up to my full 5' 8". Try to make myself look more imposing. Didn't quite pull it off.

The beefy guy turned to the others. "Someone like that can beat Collins and we are afraid of him? Come on." He said contemptuously.

'Someone like that?' Was he referring to me. This prime specimen of peak of perfection manhood? Obviously he was.

Again the heads were nodding. The beefy guy turned to me. " I'm Mick." He introduced himself and shook my hand. " Now then Dave, do you want to be a part of this or not?" he asked.

I guess I didn't have much of a choice. Besides, I did want to be part of getting rid of this particular problem.

"I'm in." I told them. "No, how are we going to go about this?"

7: The Allotment!

Finally, I was granted entrance to the select group who congregated on the path each morning. We tossed a few 'get rid of Collins ideas' around.

Ideas which got wilder, more lethal and definitely more illegal as the voices got more heated and tempers rose. Many wanted to go down and destroy Collins' allotments. Torch his sheds. I listened and finally spoke up.

"Look guys, I don't know many of you and Collins even less. But I do know that tit for tat isn't going to work. We damage his property and then what? He's just going give up and go? I don't think so. It's more likely that he will just get even. Is that what you want? An all out war?"

Everyone looked at me. Great, me and my big mouth. Lynne is always telling me to mind my own business. Stay out of trouble.

"Well, what do you suggest?" Mick, the beefy guy, asked. " Just ignore him. Let him get away with it?"

"No, I'm not saying that. But do we want to involve the council with this? If we start a war down here, it will get involved. It has no choice. And, if what I have heard is correct, Collins already has someone on the council in his pocket?".

There were nods of agreement all round. " That's right." Pete agreed. " My niece works for the council. Not in Parks and Leisure but she has a friend in that department. Word is that Collins has the ear of the deputy manager, John Burns. The suspicion is that Collins has something on him.

Nobody knows what but Burns is frightened of him. That's why any complaints about Collins just get shelved or buried."

There were further collective nods and "that's rights". Again everyone looked at me. I was beginning to feel like the sacrificial goat being introduced to the guy with the big knife.

"Ok, so we have to make him leave of his own accord. No council, no violence." I was making this up as I went. "What else do we know about him? His home life, pubs, girl friends, anything?"

"Well, he lives in Dunchurch and got turfed out of the Dunchurch allotments. Doesn't seem to have a wife or girl friend. There was talk of a woman living with him but she seems to have moved on. No visible job. His whole life seems to be wrapped up with his allotments. He drives a tatty van to and from Dunchurch to here at least twice a day. Anyone else anything further to add?" another guy chipped in."

Just then there was the clear sound of the main gate bolt being drawn. Everyone's head swiveled round. The object of our discussion had just entered the allotment. He stopped, looked up at us for a couple of minutes then carried on to his plot.

It was almost funny how quickly the group cleared. One minute they wanted blood, the next to disappear.

"Have a think about it guys." I called out to their departing backs.

*****

"It's that new guy that's stirring up the trouble." Mick told Collins. "They think that just because he beat you up….."

Mick's voice dropped off as he realised what he had just said. He was a little bantam of a guy. Small, puffed up chest, strutting around and seriously scared of the man standing in front of him.

So scared that, when Collins "asked" him to keep him updated on any new developments on the Top end, he instantly agreed.

"Listen, you little runt." Collins laid his hand on the runt's shoulder and started to squeeze. Mick started to squirm. Collins increased the pressure. This is what he liked. People scared of him.

"He didn't beat me up. I started to swing a punch that would have sent him into the middle of next week and I slipped. Then he used some sneaky Ninja move to get me down and started kicking me. I still could have taken him but I wanted him to think I was scared of him. Get him off guard so I could sort him out at my leisure. Got it?..." he asked giving a final squeeze before releasing the older man.

"Yes, I thought it must have been something like that." Mick replied rubbing his shoulder to get the feeling back.

"Right, so what was the gossip group about? The one that broke up so quickly when I came through the gate."

"The guys were angry about what happened to old Albert's plot......"

"Nothing to do with me. Some vandal must have broke in and done it." Collins smirked. " So......?"

"Well, nothing really. They were talking about how best to get rid of you. That it was no good getting onto the council because you have a mate there. The new guy, he's called Dave by the way, was saying that tit for tat wouldn't work. Nothing much was decided before they broke up. Honest, I don't know any more...."

"Yeah, well, when you do, you tell me and quickly. Any plans involving me I want to hear about. You understand?"

Mick nodded his head vigorously.

"Good, now bugger off and remember what I said. Anything at all, ok?"

Collins wandered back to his plot. So, he thought, they want me off do they? Time to ramp it up a bit. He was almost smiling as he opened up his larger shed.

I smiled as I saw Collins go into his shed. I had watched the whole incident from the entrance to the little spinney leading to the back gate. I had pretended to leave after the group broke up. I stopped at Little Mick's plot and shouted "See you" to where he was digging at the top of his plot.

He waved back and I proceeded to the gate, made a lot of noise opening and closing it then went back down towards the allotments. Ten minutes later, I saw Mick come to his plot gate as Collins called him down. I made sure I couldn't be seen and listened to every word.

I wasn't surprised. I had seen the little guy in long conversations with Collins before and sort of guessed what was going on. I tended to watch what I said around Mick from then on. Unless I wanted it to get back to Collins.

Now he thought that I was going to play fair and square. No tit for tat. Yeah, right. I was smiling as I made my way home. So much mischief, so little time.

But, before going home, I made another call. By counting the houses from the allotment, I had a good idea of where Adrian, from Plot 8, lived. I went round to what I thought was his bungalow's front door. Rang the bell and waited. It wasn't the right house. Adrian lived next door, his neighbour told me.

This time he did come to the door. "Got a minute?" I asked him. He stood aside to let me in. I was in a narrow hallway that led straight down to a kitchen.

"Go on down. Fancy a cuppa?"

"Sounds good." I told him as I looked out the window. No wonder he knew what went on down the allotment. It was almost like having a grandstand view in as much as his kitchen window looked down on the plots.

"So, I guess it's about Collins?" Adrian asked. He was a smallish guy around my age. Sharp features and inquisitive eyes. Distinctive thick white hair. I guessed he spent a lot of time looking out his kitchen window. He handed a cup of tea over.

I told him about what I had just witnessed. He nodded.

"Not surprised. I sort of guessed as much. So what do you have in mind?"

" How many of the top plot guys do you know and trust. Really trust to keep quiet?"

He sipped his tea as he thought about it. Then pointed out the window. "Pete, Paul, Big Mick and now you, I guess." He said as he indicated the plots. "The others have been here a long time so we know each other pretty well. The rest of them come and go. Actually we had bets on how long you would stay. Can't be easy putting up with Geoffrey?"

I smiled. "Naw, Geoff's ok once you get to know him. Besides, the amount of money he's spent on his plot makes my work a lot easier. I don't really see much of him. I pretty much do what I like."

"Yes, I notice he spends a lot of time in his shed with his gardener. They are probably planning crop rotation, planting and stuff like that, right?"

Not a lot got past this guy. "Do you have their phone numbers?"

He took my empty cup to the sink. "Yes, why?" he asked as he washed both cups and put them on the draining rack. Like me, he was well trained.

"I had the thought of just a small group of people getting together and sorting out Collins. Meet away from here and not let on to the others. Get some sort of idea of what we are going to do. But, also arrange meetings with the other Top enders on site. Toss ideas around and feed false information back to Collins." Adrian was nodding vigorously.

"That way we, as a sort of inner group, can plan the serious stuff without it getting back to him. What do you think? Too ambitious, too much bother, …what?"

He didn't have to think too long. "Yes, I think it's a great idea. And, about time too. We have moaned about Collins and his bully boy tactics for too long without actually doing anything about it. I guess what he did to old Albert's plot was the final straw. Time to get rid, I think."

"Yeah, well that's why I am here. Get it done and get him off. The hard way or the soft way? Legal or otherwise?" I queried.

"Give me your number and I'll ring you when I get my end sorted." Adrian said with confidence. " And, as to what way, any way that gets the best results. I don't care and I don't think the other will be too bothered either. I'll be in touch." He escorted me to the front door. As I was leaving, he held out his hand. "Good to have you on board Dave. I feel we are going to work well together."

I shook his hand. "Count on it. Working together, how hard can it be to get rid of him?"

As it turned out, harder than we thought. A lot harder.

8: The Allotment!

I live literally ten minutes from the allotment. So I was soon entering my kitchen. *"I'm home, woman. Drop whatever you are doing and feed me. And be quick about it."*

Yeah, right. Not until I have had at least two brave pills and a clear exit. "I'm back, love. Can I make you a cup of tea? Something to eat?"

Lynne came into the kitchen. "You're late. I expected you ages ago. Forget the time or something?"

"Nah, just busy." I told her about my non- existent digging and planting. She just nodded. I sometimes think that I am not fooling her.

That afternoon, I tackled my To Do list. Just when I thought I was getting on top of it, Lynne always seemed to add another job or three or four to it.

One hour later and the gate at the top of the path doesn't sag anymore. It was just a nuisance anyway. Nobody bothered to close it after them. Much better off without it. Another job off the List.

I have a big shed at the end of the garden. I call it my workshop. The whole nerve centre, Command Module of the household. Lynne calls it a Man Cave. Whatever, it is where the work gets done and I get to think without interruption.

I have a cd player and a smallish – only 23" – tv installed. I selected the BBC's news channel and sat down in my chair.

Don't worry, it's an old chair, nothing fancy. Just a leather recliner rescued from the house when Lynne went on yet another manic decorating exercise. Why slapping on a bit of paint and hanging new wallpaper automatically includes new furniture, I just don't get.

Anyway, I must have accidentally pushed the recline button because, before I knew it, I was stretched out listening to the news.

"Hey, wake up, you've got visitors." Lynne was standing in the doorway.

"I wasn't asleep." I protested. "Just resting my eyes and thinking."

"Huh, I don't know how you could rest and think with all that snoring going on. Shall I bring them up or are you coming down?"

Too late. My visitors had already followed her. Adrian, Big Mick –as opposed to Little Mick the grass – Peter and Paul. I looked around for Mary but couldn't see her. (Don't worry if you didn't get it; old timer joke.)

"Hi guys. Come in. Want a drink or anything?" After a few of those 'only if you're making one' or 'if you're having one' mumbles that people make instead of coming straight out with a Yes or No, I sent Lynne off with the orders. With a bravado that I would probably suffer for later, I called after her. "And, don't be too long about it, woman."

I could see they were impressed. They stood there shaking their heads in awe and wonderment. Or was it pity?

I look at my space invaders. I realised I wasn't sure of their names. I asked them to introduce themselves:

Adrian Miles, Plot 8: small, smart, good head of snow white hair, inquisitive eyes and a smile always twitching.

Big Mick McAvoy: The beefy guy from Plot 12. Around 35, overweight, almost bald head closely cropped with a belligerent attitude.

Pete Wills: Plot 3. Retirement age or over, tall, stout, ruddy complexion and an enviable mane of greying swept back hair.

Paul Tiler . Plot 15: Hard to describe. One of those anonymous guys. Middle aged, average height, bald head covered by a flat cap.

It was getting a bit crowded in the shed so I lead them down to the decking.

This was the latest of my home improvements. It was a 3m x3m area with balustrades. We looked at having one done by decking specialists but I decided a DIY kit was the way to go. More personal, a lot cheaper and the satisfaction of having done it all yourself.

I unstacked the plastic chairs and set them out. Warned Big Mick not to lean on the balustrade as I "hadn't quite finished it yet." I could see them all eyeing it enviously. Warily? Fearfully? Whatever. When it is finished it will be great. Number 22 on the To Do list.

Lynne came out of the french windows with a tray of tea things. Set it down on the table and left. I hadn't dismissed her but decided to let it go.

By mutual consent I was appointed Mother and set about taking orders. Things went fine until I got to Paul.

"How do you like it Paul?

"I don't know."

"Well, how do you usually take it?"

"I don't know. Sort of a dark brown with some sugar. The wife usually makes it." Said Mr Macho

Eventually we arrived at something like the right colour and sweetness.

"I rang the guys and they wanted a meet right away." Adrian started off. " I rang that mobile number you gave me but it must have been switched off. So we came on the off-chance you were in."

*****

Mobile phones are a bit of an issue in our house. I hate them and can't see the need to be in constant reach and communication. I carry one because the family make me "in case you have an accident or something".

I don't know why they have to be constantly updated for the very latest technology. I've had mine since 1986 and it still works perfectly. Good solid construction. Built to last

Granted it's a tad heavy and its brick shape doesn't allow for easy access. Otherwise, I reckon it'll see me out. Why would anyone want to in constant 24/7 touch anyway?

And, don't get me started on Facebook or Twatter. I don't have many friends but at least I have met them. My grandson informed me the other day that he has 2702 'friends'. I wouldn't want his birthday card list.

*****

"Anyway," he continued "they all thought it was a good idea. Keep the group small and contained."

Everyone's head started nodding like those little Churchill dogs people keep on their dashboards. Oh Yes.

"You told them about Little Mick?"

"Yes, we sort of guessed anyhow." Pete replied for them all. " I bet there are a couple of others as well."

"Who's in favour of sorting them out?" Big Mick asked with the light of battle shining in his eyes.

Actually no-one seemed to be. Behind him I could see Adrian rolling his eyes in a sort of "Sorry but he will be useful" gesture.

I waited for someone else to take the lead but there were no volunteers. Great, down to me again. "First of all, we have to sort out just how we are going to set about this. The hard way or the clever way?"

Paul finally spoke. "Why do we have to have choices? Why can't we just wreck his plots and then have a quiet word with him?" he asked. He hit his left palm with a fist to demonstrate his version of a quiet word.

Not surprisingly, Big Mick nodded his agreement. I could see that this wasn't going to be easy.

"If you thought it was that simple, why haven't you done it already? Just go down and batter him while you are explaining the error of his ways to him. Do you really think that would work?"

I looked around. Adrian and Pete were shaking their heads. Paul and Mick were still undecided. I waited for someone else to take over. There were no takers.

"If the police were called in, and Collins looks like the sort to do that, then the council would have to be involved as well. Even if he doesn't and decides to deal with things his way then things will get out of hand. It could end in destruction and vandalism on both sides. You damage his stuff, he does it back. The whole thing could just escalate." I tried to explain.

"If that happens then the Parks and Open Spaces office might think that a clean sweep of all the trouble makers was the best course of action. Do you really want that?"

This time all the heads were nodding. Oh Yes. I took a sip of tea before continuing.

"Basically, as I see it, we need to get him to leave voluntarily. We can either make him think it was his idea or we can make things so difficult for him that he decides it isn't worth the effort. Either way we are going to have to be clever and take our time."

"Ok" Mick broke first. "What do you suggest?" I looked at them.

"Well, first of all, why does it have to be me to suggest everything? I thought the whole idea of you coming here was to work out a joint way of dealing with him. You've all known him longer than I have. You must have some ideas of your own?"

"You have been the only one to face him down and beat him." Adrian pointed out. "Maybe we were just waiting for someone like you to come and help us." Oh Yes. Oh Yes, Oh Yes. Quite a breeze getting up there.

"Right." I decided enough was enough for now. I was already beginning to regret getting involved. "Look, the best thing is for everyone to go home, have a good think and come up with a plan. A plan that doesn't involve fists or fire. Something based on your knowledge of the bloke. Then we meet up again and see what everyone has come up with. Anyone got any ideas for a meeting place?" I looked around.

"I don't mind you coming here but it is a main road and sooner or later someone is going to see you all traipsing up the road together and put two and two together."

They all decided to have a think about it and decide a suitable meeting place. Meeting adjourned, gentlemen.

9: The Allotment!

"What was all that about?" was the first question after I had seen them out. "Who is this Collins bloke anyway?" was the second. I hadn't noticed that the staff had left the french window partly open.

Which left me in a quandary. I don't like keeping things from Lynne. I'm not that partial to the pain and grief that follows after she finds out I have been keeping secrets. Time to come clean.

After I had told her everything, apart from Geoff and his gardener, she gave me her considered opinion.

"Oh, I thought it might be about Geoff and his fancy piece."

"You know about that? How?" I hadn't said anything. What happens down the allotment stays down the allotment, right? "Who told you?"

"Geoff's wife. She has known about it for ages. She's all for it. Keeps him from bothering her."

"Oh." So much for secrets. "Well, what do you think about getting rid of Collins? Any ideas?"

"Actually I think your idea was the best." she said grudgingly. "Get him to leave on his own accord. That way there will be no comeback afterwards. I'm sure the council, particularly his contact in the office, will be pleased." She then deftly changed the subject.

"By the way, where does that Adrian live? Is he single? I just love all that snow white hair. Why can't you have white hair?" she asked with a serious face.

Adrian, and his white hair, was down the allotment when I arrived the next morning.
I knocked on the door before going into Geoff's shed. Didn't want to disturb him. I hadn't seen him for a few days. I'd have to ask Lynne where he was.

Adrian followed me in after first checking that there was no-one down the Lower end. He had a good look around, taking it all in. He grinned and shook his head.

"Right, I spoke to the guys afterwards and they agreed that you should run things. We kicked a few ideas around and no-one came up with anything better so we are going with your ideas." He informed me with a grin on his face.

"What about a meeting place? Any ideas on that or do I have to sort that out as well?"

He missed, or ignored, the sarcasm. "Oh, no. That was no problem. There is a pub called the Red Lion in Crick. We'll meet there, as and when. It's out of the way and the opposite side of Rugby to Collins."

A pub? What an unexpected location. "Anything else?"

"We thought we should have a few group meetings down here. With as many of the others as can come. That way we can feed false information to Collins. It wouldn't hurt to accidentally drop a few things to Little Mick as well. I'm sure Collins has other people looking out for him as well but we don't want to make it too obvious."

"Can't argue with that." I agreed. "Now, we need info on his personal life. Where he lives, what he does for money, where he goes, friends enemies, that sort of thing. Know anyone who lives near him?"

"One of the other guys has a relative with a plot on his last allotment. I'll get him to have a quiet word. Other than that, you probably know his movements to and from the allotment as well as anyone. " He caught my inquiring look. "You know, looking out the window. He comes down the main road from Dunchurch and must go past your house every time."

I shook my head. I had no idea what sort of vehicle he drove. I said as much to Adrian.

"Oh, I thought you knew. Right, he lives in Dunchurch. Used to have an allotment there until he got kicked off." He saw my enquiring look. "It wasn't run by Rugby Borough council. A committee ran it and got fed up of Collins thinking that rules didn't apply to him. He's been on our patch for the last five years." He thought a bit more.

"Transport. He drives an old Vauxhall van. White with a tatty Remembrance Poppy on the front grille. Back windows are blacked out but with two yellow stickers on either side. That's about it for what I know. We'll have to ask the others at our first meet."

I asked when that was likely to be. I wasn't surprised to hear that it was scheduled for 9-ish tomorrow evening.

"In the meantime, if you see the others, tell them to have a think about Collins. What they know, what they suspect, any ideas they might have."

I was suddenly getting that 'what have I let myself in for?' feeling. Was there going to be more sinking than thinking?

I wasn't that comfortable in pubs. I hardly ever drank anything stronger than tea or coffee by choice. Alcohol was not something I had acquired a taste for. In fact, it was the taste that put me off in the first place.

Lynne liked a drop of wine and often tried to get me to taste test with her. I must have funny taste buds – probably destroyed after all those cigarettes – because wine always tastes like vinegar to me. I might just as well be drinking a glass of Sarsons.

As for spirits they taste funny as well. Funny as in screwing my face up and wanting to spit it out funny. Beer and lager the same. People tell me if I persevere I will get used to it. I really can't see the point of that.

So, for me, pubs are places to endure. To pretend that I like alcohol fumes being breathed on me. To be the only one not getting the joke or remark that has my companions laughing hysterically. To be automatically being labelled as the Designated Driver.

Well, they wouldn't be getting any Designated Driving in my Landcruiser that was for sure.

Basically I wasn't looking forward to our meeting at The Red Lion in Crick but couldn't see anyway of getting out of it.

I still wanted to get rid of the joint problem but would have preferred to do it over a latte than a lager.

Still, brave little soldier that I was, I would give it a go.

10: The Allotment!

Bert Collins whistled to himself as he finished his task. He was inside his big shed as opposed to his smaller one on the adjoining plot. His face creased into a rare smile as he looked at the finished product.

It was a candle stuck in a ball of mud. Halfway down the candle he had wound a twist of green gardeners string. The fluffy kind used for tying up plants, raspberries and the like. Next to this was a plastic one pint milk container with the string ends threaded through two of the three holes in the blue cap.

The container was nearly full of petrol and the two pieces of string were hanging in the liquid. Already the string was acting like a wick and drawing up the petrol. Soon the soaked string would travel down to and around the candle.

Knowing from previous experience that it would work, he removed the pieces of string and put the components of his home made igniter to one side. Once the strings were in place again and the candle lit, he estimated he had around twenty minutes to get home and establish his alibi.

After that time the candle would have burned down to the wrapped petrol soaked string and set it alight. The flames would travel up the string and ignite the fumes coming from the holes in the milk container cap. The resultant explosion would send the petrol flying and ignite anything in its path.

Simple, yet effective, with the evidence of his ignition system destroyed in the ensuing fireball.

For now though, there were too many people around and it was too light. He preferred darkness to set off his timer.

In the meantime, he saw that the latest newcomer was ineffectively digging away in one corner of his overgrown allotment. Time to make a new friend and ally.

Grabbing his fork and shovel he ambled down and introduced himself. Within minutes he was alongside the sweating newcomer and digging busily. Hard work but worth it to create the impression he wanted.

As they dug companionably together, he quickly found out all he wanted to know about the newcomer. As always he stored it away for future use.

Soon the amount of newly dug earth was looking impressive. With the light beginning to fade it was agreed to call it a day. With the heart felt thanks of his new friend ringing in his ears, Collins returned to his shed.

Waiting until the newcomer had left, he looked around the allotments but could see no one else in the gathering darkness. Time to move.

Gathering his equipment, he walked up the path and towards the Top End. He continued walking until he was halfway down the path and then turned into an allotment on his left.

After another look round, he approached the shed and inserted a pry bar behind the screws on the hasp. A quick wrench and the hasp and padlock fell to one side. He knelt down and retrieved the four screws from where they had fallen. He put them in his pocket within easy reach. Opening the door he entered and quickly set up his homemade timer and bomb.

Satisfied he had left a big enough distance between the milk container and flame he carefully lit the candle and withdrew. Holding the hasp in place he pushed the four screws into their original positions.

Once again it looked as if the shed was locked and undisturbed. Probably overkill as the shed would be burnt to ashes but, like the bomb and timer, undetectable afterwards.

More quickly now, he returned to his van, started the engine and drove away. As he turned into the main road, he saw one of the allotment holders washing his car on his drive. Pipping his horn, he waved as he drove past. Perfect, another alibi established. Now all he had to do was make sure his neighbours saw him going into his house, before the fire started, and he was in the clear.

Whistling happily to himself, he drove home as quickly as possible. Let battle commence.

11: The Allotment!

The next morning I was in town with Lynne. We had been shopping and, as a special treat, I had decided to treat her to a meal.

We don't go out much since I retired and she missed the lavish press do's we used to attend together.

Rugby couldn't offer much to compete with the swanky hotels and restaurants we went to in those heady days but I took her to the best place in town.

I fussed over her as I sat her down. Made sure she was comfortable. I knew what she would like so I ordered for us both. The service was quick and soon our meal was in front of us.

She tucked in with relish. She does love her Mac Muffin Breakfast Meal. I had ordered all the trimmings. Hash browns, beans and a nice cup of tea. No expense spared for my Lynne.

Just as I had started, my mobile rang. I ignored it as I usually do. Truth be told, I didn't realise it was my phone ringing. I must have accidentally switched it on before leaving home. Lynne asked me if I was going to answer it.

I tugged it out of my coat pocket, pressed the button and held it to my ear. Almost instantly, I could feel the envious glances as the other diners spotted my phone.

A couple of teenagers a few tables down pointed and burst out laughing. Other people were grinning broadly. A few more looked on in total disbelief. Envy effects people in many different ways I suppose.

It was Adrian with the White Hair. We spoke for a few minutes. "Ok, I'll get down as soon as I can." I promised him. "I'm in town at the moment so it'll be a while." I listened some more. "Well it isn't going to make much difference now, is it?" I switched off and looked at Lynne.

I answered her unspoken question. "It was Adrian with the White Hair. The shed on the Geoff's allotment has burnt down."

*****

It was a good two hours before I got down to the allotment. There didn't seem any point in hurrying.

From what Adrian had told me it had happened late yesterday evening. The Fire Brigade had been called but couldn't do much other than stand around and make sure it didn't spread.

"I spotted it around 9.30 last night." Adrian explained. "I thought at first it was someone burning rubbish. That guy from Plot 21 likes to burn his rubbish in the evening. Saves him carting it down to the skip."

The council provide a skip for people to put their allotment waste into. Many of us use it to get rid of hedge clippings, grass, leaves and such like from their homes.

"Anyway." Adrian continued. " I called the Fire Brigade but they couldn't do much. They couldn't bring their truck up here and by the time they had stretched their hoses up here, it would have been too late anyhow."

That much was obvious. There was hardly anything left of Geoff's love nest.

The skeletal remains of the bed, the fused mass of electronics that had been a tv and a radio and the heat distorted cooking ring. A few charred roof timbers, some of the door and a little bit of the back wall.

Surprisingly, the gas cylinder that fuelled the gas ring was blackened but otherwise intact.

" The fire bloke said it was a fierce burn that was over in a very short time. Everything was tinder dry so it burnt quickly. The cylinder didn't have enough time to heat up before the fire had burnt itself out. Just as well, he reckoned those cylinders go off like bombs once they explode." Adrian scratched his white head underneath all that white hair.

"They had a good look round but couldn't see anything obvious. There was no way of saying how it had started. The padlock was still locked in the hasp. He had been out to the last shed that got burnt here and there was nothing at that one either. He reckoned that people are either very careless or we have an arson problem. Other than report to the police there wasn't anything else for us to do."

Several of the other guys had come up once they saw what had happened. Big Mick was all for getting some petrol and setting light to Collins' shed.

"Hold on." Said an older guy called Ron. "I assume you think that Bert Collins is responsible." Several heads nodded. Ron turned to Adrian. "Did I hear you say you first spotted it at 9.30 last night?"

Adrian nodded his white hair. "Yes, I was doing the washing up and looking out at the plots. I was thinking how nice some of them looked. Next minute there was a noise and I saw flames coming out the window of the shed.

I guess the noise I heard was tied into the shed burning. What I can't understand is that the Fire bloke said there was no obvious suspicious signs that it had been started deliberately. I didn't see anyone running away either so that is a bit of a head scratcher."

"Well, I was washing my car last night around nine. It was getting dark but there was nothing on the telly." Ron continued. "Bert Collins went past and pipped his horn. I thought then that the guy can't have any home life. But, if the shed went up at 9.30 and I saw Collins at 9 then how could it have been him?"

This caused other arguments but no one could get past the facts as Ron had seen them. No-one doubted what he had seen but no-one could come up with an explanation for Collins still being the arsonist either.

Big Mick was still angry. He took Adrian and myself to one side. "We need to meet and talk about this." He muttered. "Tonight at Crick around 9?" He didn't wait for an answer but stomped back down to his plot.

"Well, he has a point. I'll tell the others. Best if we go separately and meet up there?" Adrian asked as he returned to his plot.

"Yeah, good plan guys. I'll see you then" I muttered under my breath. Just then another thought struck me. Had anyone told Geoff? He wasn't going to be best pleased, was he?

Geoff wasn't pleased. He had opened the door and seen who was calling. I still hadn't completely figured Geoff out. Some times he was friendly and almost likeable. Other times, like now, he looked at me like something he had stepped in.

He had stepped out and closed the door. "What?" he asked almost angrily. " I'd rather you didn't call here. What is it that can't wait until we are down the allotment?"

I really did think about turning round and walking away or just tapping him with my fist. I am not normally violent unless provoked and, just now, Geoff was provoking me.

"Pardon me for calling unannounced. For some reason I thought you might be interested to hear that your shed was burnt to the ground last night. I'm sorry for having disturbed you. I'll see you down the allotment sometime." I was halfway down the path before he caught up with me.

"Wait, wait, Look , I am sorry ok. You just caught me at a bad moment." Some emotion played across his face. I could see he was thinking about something. After a moment he just blurted out "I was having a row with my wife, if you must know. It was getting rather heated. I think she suspects what is going on. Sorry. About the shed?"

Tell him or not? I had nothing to lose so decided to let him know that his wife already knew about his affair. He looked at me with staring eyes and mouth open.

"What? What? She can't. We have been so careful." He stammered. Then his expression changed as he thought it through. "Ok, that does make things a bit clearer. How does she know? Did you tell her?"

"No, Geoff, I didn't. Why would I?" I then told him what Lynne had told me. How his wife knew about his 'fancy piece' and was glad because it meant that he wasn't 'bothering' her any more. " I gather she had known for some time."

His shoulders slumped and I actually felt sorry for him. "Look, about the shed. It was burnt down last night. Everyone thinks it was Collins but he was seen leaving around 9 and Adrian saw the shed go up at 9.30. So that makes it difficult to prove. Has anyone else got a grudge against you? Were you down there last night and left something burning?"

He shook his head vigorously. "No. I haven't been down for a couple of days now. And I can't think of anybody else down there who would do it. It's payback for you beating him up, isn't it?"

"Well, that's what everyone is saying but, given his alibi, that is in doubt. The fire guys found nothing to suggest it was deliberate. I wasn't in the shed yesterday. You weren't. The padlock was still attached to the door hasp and locked. You tell me how it was done."

I looked at him. He seemed lost in thought. Dejected looking with sagging shoulders and a bewildered look in his eyes.

I told him to have a look at the remains of the shed and have another think about it. We'd have a chat next time we were down there together. He didn't even look up as I left.

Back home I told Lynne about the
shed, Geoff and Collins' apparent alibi.
"What about your cameras?" she
asked. " Won't he be on one of them?"

Good thinking Batwoman. The old
dear has her uses sometimes. I should
have thought about my security
cameras myself.

*****

Our house is a corner plot. It means
we get more land but extra problems
as well.

The front of the house is on the main
road. The side is on Maple Road. A
hedge starts at the now missing front
gate and follows the road around. At
the end of the hedge is our garage and
open parking area. A path from the
house leads across the garden and to
the garage. But, and this is the
problem, the garage and parking area
can't be seen from the house.

I mentioned that I used to be a transport journalist right? Part of my job was testing trucks. But I also tested diesel engined vans and cars as well. These were delivered to my house and left for a week. They had a full tank of fuel and there was no obligation to return them with a full tank.

Basically they were mine for a week and I used them as such. The obligation being that I would write a comprehensive and accurate road test of the vehicle and how I felt about it.

It was a win win situation. I got paid for the road tests by the various magazines I wrote for. I had a free vehicle for a week and I used it for my work. The magazines I wrote for were charged the usual 35 pence a mile travelling expense involved in getting the article they had commissioned. So I liked having these free vehicles.

Unfortunately, some of the people walking past my garage and parking area got a bit peeved at seeing me with yet another brand new vehicle. Knowing they couldn't be seen from the house they sometimes vented their anger, jealousy, whatever, by damaging the vehicle. Keying down the sides, smashing lights or slashing tyres.

What began as isolated incidents became more regular and, as a consequence, the vehicle owners began to question whether this van/cardalism was worth it.

Hence the cameras.

I contacted the police after every incident. This was to safeguard me and to provide a police incident reference number to the vehicle owner for insurance purposes. It was the local Community Support Officer who first mentioned getting a camera.

The first one was a basic black and white one. I set it up out of sight and watched on a monitor beneath the tv. It was fine during the day but useless at night. I upgraded to a night vision camera and this was good at night. But I then had to have a means of recording the footage so a vhs recorder joined the monitor.

One morning I went to my latest van and found two flat tyres. I went back to the house and checked the recorded footage. It showed a neighbour sticking something into both tyres. I called the police and showed the tape. I was told that the actual footage was no use because it was not date and time stamped. However they did have a word with the neighbour who denied it. He said his kid's ball had rolled under the van and he was looking to retrieve it.

After that I upgraded to a top of the range system Eight camera with infra-red night vision. Five showing the garage and parking area. Every camera overlapped each other. Between them, they covered every bit of the property and any vehicle parked there. There were three more monitoring the front of the house.

All the cameras fed into a digital hard drive recorder that was connected to my computer. Supposedly I could check my security set up via the internet from my mobile. I wasn't bothered about this option as it would have meant changing my trusty mobile.

But it did mean that all eight cameras were recording and storing 24/7. I could see at a glance which cameras had been triggered by the motion sensors. The date/time stamp showed me when these recording had taken place. The local plod assured me that this was all the evidence I needed to take any vandal to court.

To date I hadn't had to use it in court. The vandalism stopped but I liked having the cameras. Sometimes I found that watching the monitor was more entertaining that watching the tv.

The reason the vandalism stopped could have been due to the large WARNING: CCTV CAMERAS IN OPERATION 24/7 signs I had prominently displayed around the rear of the house.

Equally, it could have been due to the vandalising neighbour finding four slashed tyres on his car one morning. Nothing was ever said but the attacks did stop. Maybe a coincidence?

That was a few years back but, even though I have retired, the cameras remained. They still worked well and were still entertaining sometimes.

*****

I like to think that I would have got round to checking the cameras myself. I had a time scale to work from and that made it easier. I pulled up the previous night's footage from cameras 6,7,and 8. These covered the front of the house and overlapped each other.

Lots of vehicles go up and down our main road. I selected the middle camera as giving the best view and looked at the footage recorded between 9 and 9.30 the previous evening.

Around five minutes past nine a white van went past. There was a flash of red on the grille. I paused the recorder and, using the mouse, zoomed in.

Sure enough, there was Collins in the driver's seat. He was looking across at our house, grinning and holding up two fingers.

Strangely, I was quite calm as I saved the screen shot.   I printed out a quality photo and switched the computer off.

Collins had just started something that I was going to finish.

12: The Allotment!

The Red Lion pub was on the main street in Crick.

Crick itself was one of those little country villages that hadn't changed too much. The famous Rugby radio masts were practically on its doorstep and were perhaps it's best known claim to fame.

It's most famous resident was Ken Richmond, the big, well muscled guy, who used to beat the gong -made of paper incidentally- before the start of the Rank films.

It was in the late 70's that it started to grow. Mainly because of the M1 and M6 motorways on its doorsteps which provided excellent commuter routes.

But the village councillors were united in their desire to keep the village as small as possible. Consequently it hadn't grown as much as similar villages had. And, those developments that were allowed, were in keeping with the original buildings.

But the real death knell of this once sleepy little village was the building of the Daventry International Rail Freight terminal (DIRFT) on the other side of the M1 motorway.

This was started in '97 and has been growing ever since. In it's wake it experienced a surge of labour requirements. So, despite the councillors best efforts, the village had expanded to accommodate more and more DIRFT workers.

But, inside the Red Lion, time had, if
not stood still, resisted the all
enveloping changes going on around
it. The nicotine stained ceiling, time
etched beams and antique feel were all
real. There was no sawdust on the
flagged floor but you felt like there
ought to be.

It remained a traditional and
genuine village pub and was well
frequented and much loved by its
customers.

I had come in Lynne's little car. It
was too small to become the
Designated Driver's vehicle. I parked it
at one end of a fairly busy car park. I
looked for the one horse that villages
like this usually boasted but couldn't
see it.

Maybe it was on a date with one of
the villagers?

The group I had come to see were gathered in a corner. Judging by the number of empty glasses on the table, they had arrived some time before.

I hadn't dressed up for the occasion and, I was relieved to see, neither had they. Paradoxically, for a little village pub, most of the customers were wearing suits and/or designer casuals.

A few old timers, in traditional yokel dress, were in chairs around the lit fire. Some were playing some sort of game with wooden blocks and matches. A couple had unlit pipes surgically attached to their mouths. No obvious sign of spittoons but you never knew.

It wasn't cold enough for the fire but, hey, it was traditional. And, it did create a nice cosy atmosphere.

Occasionally, one of these old timers would shuffle to the bar and hand over a few eggs or similar for a pint.

Every now and then an old newcomer would appear and this usually resulted in deep laughter and some shaky high sixes as he joined the Oldtimers group.

For some reason I do not perceive myself as old. I feel young in my head so assume I look the same. Sometimes it is quite a shock to see a doddery old man in some shop window and, belatedly, realise it is me. So, although I called them old they probably only had a few years on me.

As a non-drinker, I had to establish some rules regarding buying drinks. Buying a round of pints when you drink a soft drink quickly became counter-expensive. So, as soon as I had sat down, I explained my position.

"No problem." Big Mick replied. " We already decided we would all buy our own drinks. So get your milk in and join us."

As I said, they already had a few inside them so this was laughed at uproariously. I ordered a half pint of lemonade with just enough beer in it to add a 'proper' drink colour.

It tended to distract the attention and the subsequent derogatory remarks away from the fact that I was a secret lemonade drinker.

They were already discussing everything but the purpose for coming here. I sort of guessed this would happen. It usually does. I quickly brought the subject up. "Has anyone had any constructive thoughts about Collins?"

"Yes" Big Mick told me. " I say we knock him out, put him in his shed and set light to it. That should solve the problem."

"Anything less drastic? Have any of you found out what he does in his spare time? Women, sex, pub....anything?"

"I know where he lives in Dunchurch." Paul contributed. "He lives in one of those council houses off the Dunchurch Road. I don't know the number but it is the last one on the right on Moot Lane."

"Well, that's good. Anything else?" I looked around. "Have you been there? Does he live alone, married, girl friend or what?"

"I went there about a year ago." Paul continued. "I did some work on his van for him. I was a mechanic before I retired." He added for this my benefit. "He didn't pay me right away and, when I asked for it, he just told me to bugger off. I didn't see anyone else in the house. I went in to use the toilet but it was in a right mess. I would guess from the state of it that he lives alone.

But there was talk of a woman living with him for some time. Apparently she just left one day and didn't come back. It was rumored that Collins was just a bit too handy with his fists. I never did get paid. Not even for the brake discs." He told us bitterly.

"Paul, I don't think you are going to get that money. " Adrian told him. " I have been observing Collins for a while now. Not deliberately but I see a lot from my house. He goes out of his way to make friends with any newcomers. The lower end rather than our end. I don't know but I have heard he is trying to get some sort of Association going. With him in control, of course."

"Yeah, he got kicked out of his last allotment by the Association running it and I reckon that is his ultimate aim. Set up an Association and make himself bulletproof." Pete chipped in.

The conversation sort of died up then. I surmised what we knew. "So, he lives alone in Dunchurch, drives to the allotment twice a day in a white van and wants to get control. That about sum it up? It's not much to work with is it? Anybody know anything about his contact at the Town hall?"

Pete shrugged his shoulders. " My niece works there. It's the deputy manager, John Burns, in the Parks and Open Spaces department.

Other than the fact that he is scared of Collins, she hasn't been able to find anything out. I've told her to keep trying." He added.
I decided that was enough for the night. I had found out very little about Collins that wasn't general knowledge.

On the other hand I had found out that Paul used to be a mechanic. I always like to know a good mechanic. They tended to be useful. I wondered what they other did or used to do. I asked the question.

Big Mick was a van driver on parcel deliveries for a firm at DIRFT. He used to be a truck driver for Eddie Stobart but health problems – an ever increasing waistline - had meant the change to a smaller vehicle and less hectic employment.

Pete was an ex engineer. He used to work for a large local engineering company that moved elsewhere. He was offered alternative employment but opted for the redundancy money instead. He had been with the company since school so got a good settlement figure. He used this to set up a locksmith company. He was already into clocks, locks and similar stuff as a hobby so decided to turn it into a paying proposition.

Apparently he was quite successful and the company with 10 vans on call-out, 30 staff and a trade and retail outlet was now run by his son.

Adrian with his white hair was a retired accountant. He didn't elaborate other than to say it was for a big, well known company and he handled several large and prestigious accounts.

In return, I sketched in my history. Driver, owner driver, journalist, development driving specialist, editor and now skilled handyman.

They didn't seem that overwhelmed. Time to call it a night? With a reminder to have a think about Collins, to find his weak spots and to come up with a workable plan each, I left them to it.

Big Mick stopped me just before I left. Squinting up at me, he belched beer fumes into my face, grinned and said, "You....you're all right, you are Dave. Even if you don't drink. But... but I have a question....." His face worked furiously as he tried to remember what it was...."Oh, I know.... I was just thinking we ought to have a name. A special secret name that only we know. We ought to call ourselves something, right?"

I pretended to give it serious consideration. Why did we need a name? Just them my weird sense of humour took over and flashed a name into my head.

"Yes, I think you're right Mick. We need a name. Why don't we call ourselves the Allotmenteers? You know, one for all and all for one. What do you reckon?" He missed the sarcasm.

He considered it with that long deliberation of the drunk. He ground his teeth, bared his lips, ran his tongue over them, sighed deeply.

"Perfick. Just perfick." He smiled around the table. " That's good isn't it, boys. The five Allotmenteers. One for all and all for one." He grinned, closed his eyes and started to snore.

I got into the car wondering how the others were going to get Big Mick home. One for all. All for one? I decided to start tomorrow.

The Allotmenteers? My sense of humour was going to get me into trouble some day. But, it did give me the beginnings of an idea of dealing with the Allotmenteers problem

13: The Allotment!

Most of my family and friends tell me I have a weird sense of humour. I don't see it but sometimes I find something very funny that other people don't.

I was trying to find an example that wasn't too extreme. My first thought took me back to when I lived briefly in Ireland as a fifteen year old.

On the next farm was an old guy who used to go to the pub every night in a donkey and cart. He got quietly drunk every night and, every night, the bar staff would load him into his cart, set the donkey loose and it would take him home.

He would rouse himself enough to get into bed and that was the end of another night out he couldn't remember. I felt more sorry for the donkey that was left outside with cart still attached.

One Halloween night myself and four local friends decided it would be a good idea to play a joke on him.

Halloween in Ireland is still regarded with suspicion and fear. It is called Pooka Night. Perfectly sane and hard hearted farmers would tell me with complete sincerity that Halloween was the 'time the fairies and pixies got their own back'.

This Halloween we waited for the old guy to arrived home, stumble into bed and then we set to work. We unhitched the donkey, took the cart apart into manageable pieces and reassembled it in his parlour. We hitched up the donkey again , left it some hay and departed.

We never saw his face the next morning but would have liked to. For some time after he was telling anyone who would listen that the pixies had done it all. He never left the donkey outside again though.

Not funny? Doesn't appeal to your sense of humour? Another example?

During my trucking days I used to buy all my diesel on the continent. Usually at a lot less than filling up in the UK.

I eventually bought a Citroen CX diesel car as well, even though diesel fuelled cars weren't that popular in England. It seemed stupid buying cheap diesel for my truck and running a petrol car.

I used to siphon diesel out of my truck's tank straight into my car. I got tax relief on my truck's fuel operating costs so I was, in effect, running my car for nothing.

My next door neighbour got interested in diesel cars after listening to me extolling their virtues. Eventually he bought one of those little Japanese three cylinder turbo diesel cars. I think it was a Daihatsu Charade but can't be that sure.

Every time he saw me after that he never failed to tell me how cheap it was to run. It came with a full tank of diesel and "I haven't even had to top it up yet." he would tell me seriously. He would tell anyone who would listen about how his car must be 'doing well over 100mpg.'

What he didn't know was that I was topping his tank up in the early hours before I set off on another weekly trip. This went on for about nine months. It didn't cost me much and it appealed to my weird sense of humour.

The car's amazing mpg continued until we moved to a bigger house. I bumped into him locally some time after and we got into the ex neighbours chat about moving, how things had changed, what his new neighbours were like and similar stuff.

Just before we went our separate ways he told me that he had a problem with his car. Apparently it had suddenly started using fuel and the dealer was at a loss to understand why.

"I told them I had never ever put any fuel in it until about two months ago but I don't think they believed me." He told me with a bewildered expression.

My weird sense of humour sometimes got me into trouble. Like the time I told a shop assistant that I was having so much fun since I had found the credit card I offered her. It was mine but it seemed like a good idea at the time. Sometimes I say things without properly thinking them through.

The store security didn't find it so funny and I had some serious explaining to do before being let go. Coincidentally , Lynne had never liked going shopping with me after that incident for some reason.

But, there was the weird sense of humour 'let's have a laugh' type and then there was the 'let's see if you have a sense of humour' really weird type.

I had the sudden thought that Albert Collins didn't have much of a sense of humour. And, that I was going to push that assumption to its limit.

14: The Allotment!

Down at the allotment the next morning, I spied Adrian and Pete having a chat. Joining them I looked around for Big Mick.

"He probably won't be here today. Not early anyway." Pete said guessing who I was looking for. "We left him at The Red Lion last night. I offered to drive him home but he decided to stay. He's either still there or else he got a taxi home. He was shouting 'The Allotmenteers! All for One and One for All' as we left. Why did you put that daft idea into his head?"

"Well, he was insisting that we call ourselves something. It just popped into my head. My sense of humour." I apologised. "Speaking of which, has Collins got one? A sense of humour, I mean. I thought of something last night after I got home."

"I've heard him laughing. When he is showing his best side he can be quite entertaining. Whether it is real or not, I don't know." Adrian offered. "He's got a Jekyll and Hyde personality. Charming and friendly one moment and kicking off the next. He seems to try to get people to like him initially then if they don't go along with him, he turns nasty and violent."

"Yes, that's how I read him." I agreed. "So, if we were to make fun of him or get people laughing at him, what would be his reaction?"

Pete and Adrian traded glances. "He wouldn't like it. He doesn't like people laughing at him." Pete said firmly.

"Nor does he like being bested. You should know that. Why do you ask?"

"What if we launched a campaign to make fun of him? Really ramped it up. Could we provoke him into something stupid?" I looked at them both.

"Are you sure you want to do that? He can go really berserk." Adrian asked with a worried frown under all that white hair.

"Well, yes I do. I know there is a risk but hopefully only to property. Once we start, we put all our best tools and stuff in Adrian's garage out of the way. Produce and sheds can be easily replaced and worth the price if we get rid of him."

"No-one's has been able to do that yet." Pete pointed out. "Why should it be any different now?"

"Because we will be doing it together. Everything he does to us, we do something to him. Nothing illegal – well not too illegal anyway – or life threatening. The objective is to get him either kicked off by the Council or to humiliate him so much he leaves of his own accord."

They looked at each other. Slowly a grin spread over Pete's face. They looked at me. Nodded. It was agreed.

"Right, leave it with me. I have some ideas. In the meantime, I am going to remove what's left of the shed. Put it on the skip." I started to walk up the path towards my plot. Stopped and turned round. "Any of you guys got any braces? Baseball caps? If you have, bring them with you tomorrow. I'll explain then."

As I walked up the path, I thought about what I had just said. MY plot. I had the thought that Geoff wouldn't be returning. Why would he? No love nest anymore. His wife knew and, apparently didn't care about his girl friend. Why keep up the allotment pretence anymore? I wouldn't push it though. Let him come to that decision himself. I hoped the Bible was right about the co-workers inheriting the earth.

I spent most of the morning clearing away the remains of the shed and burnt equipment. I barrowed what was left of the shed to the skip. The burnt tools and other equipment I piled up to the side of the main gate.

Everyone who came through that gate would see them and know what they represented. I hoped that some of those still sitting on the fence would see them and get some backbone. It was developing into one of those For Us or Against Us scenarios.

I was going to rake over the site of the shed but remembered that I didn't have a rake or any other serviceable tool. I would have to bring some of my own down from home.

I borrowed a rake from Pete and finished off the job. It was a good morning's work and I stank like a wet leaf bonfire afterwards. I was feeling tired, stinky but very positive as I walked back home.

A shower, something to eat and then go into town. I wanted to do a trawl of the charity shops. And, like most places, Rugby has more than enough to spare.

*****

I like charity shops. True there are too many and they tend to charge nearly new prices for some stuff. But I do get a lot of stuff from them.

Books for instance. I read a lot of books and tend to buy from the charity shops that sell them at fifty pence. I read the book and then take it back. Everyone wins.

I just can't see the logic in charging £1.50 upwards for a paperback and then having it sit on the shelf for ever. And, if I ignore a charity shop because it tries to sell expensive books then I don't even bother to go in to check out its other wares.

Like most older men, I don't see the point in buying new clothes. I tend to slop about in jeans and tee shirts – Myton Hospice chic – and wear my good stuff when Lynne and I go out for a meal. And, let me add, not always to McDonald's either. Sometimes we really push the boat out and go to a Harvester or KFC.

And I have some really nice and expensive Hugo Boss suits, designer shirts etc. from my journalist days and save them for 'best'.

But I am one of those people who could wear a really expensive suit and it would still look like a market knock-off and just hang on me.

So, charity shops jeans, tee shirts or pullovers at a maximum £4 -£6 are ideal for casual wear. Get them dirty or tear them, then no harm done. Discard them and buy a similar cheap replacement.

So, I was used to trawling the charity shops for specific items. The usual problem when going after something specific is that, because you want it, you can't readily find it.

But, eventually my perseverance paid off and I managed to find most of what I needed for a very reasonable outlay.

I was hoping that, along with what the other 'Allotmenteers' could supply, there was enough. The very thought of what I needed the items for brought what Lynne calls my 'you're plotting something' smile to my face.

Back home I had a quick rummage through my Nerve Centre of the Household shed. I was looking for something I had purchased some time back when I was having the vandalism problem.

Thanks to my brilliant cataloguing system I quickly found it. Even better, when I turned it on and tested it, it was working fine.

If everything went as planned, this particular item was going to be very necessary. I put everything into a hold all ready for taking down the allotment in the morning.

My last task was to phone a friend of mine and ask him something. Hopefully he had the answer or could ask someone else.

Eamon Cartier was a scrap metal merchant. He preferred to call himself a Breaker of selected vehicles but his premises still looked like a scrap yard. I had first met him some years ago when looking for a part for a car. I was into Rover SD1's back then and they weren't the most reliable of vehicles.

He was based in Northampton and I found him in Yellow Pages. For the uninitiated, that was like an early manual search engine.

When I rang him he took about a minute to tell me he had the part, what it cost and what he would charge for fitting it. I was quite capable of fitting it myself but, for the price he quoted, it wasn't worth putting on overalls and crawling under the car.

When I arrived at his yard, I found it stacked with cars of various ages, models and condition. I later found out that he had the police contract to remove abandoned cars in the area. So, apart from getting the vehicles for nothing, he also got paid to remove them.

His main source of income was buying vehicles –mot failures, insurance write-offs and the like – salvaging the useable parts and selling what remained as scrap.

For some reason we hit it off instantly. I liked roaming round scrap cars for spares and he liked the tickets I could supply for Silverstone, Donnington and other press events.

I ended up getting my spares for nothing and he got the chance to meet celebrities, drive the latest model cars and take part in the various Motor Shows and Press Days we went to.

"Hi Eamon, it's Dave Williams."
"Allo you old bugger. What you after this time?" Even though I could no longer supply as many tickets as before we still remained friends.

I told him what I was after and, as efficient as ever, he said he could supply it and deliver. I then asked if he could get hold of registration plates without the hassle of registration documents and identity.
"No problem." He assured me. "Give me the number."

" I can't until later this evening or tomorrow morning. How much time do you need?"
"Half an hour after you give me the details. Soon enough? When do you want delivery?"

I explained what I wanted the vehicle for and that I would be returning it in a couple of weeks time.

"And, don't tell me, you are not expecting to pay me anything, right?"

"No, but I will owe you one."

"Ok, tell me when and where and I'll get it to you soonest. Anything else? Want to borrow my wife, daughter, bank account details?"

Lynne and, I suspect, many other women, doesn't understand the male favour system.

Somebody does me a favour then I will owe a favour in return. It might not be immediate but, sometime in the future, I will get a call and a favour to be redeemed.

It's all done on trust and the understanding that owing a favour is like a sacred oath and you do not fail.

So when I told Eamon I owed him a favour he knew without question that I would repay it. And vice versa.

Most men understand the favour system. It makes the tough male world work just that little bit easier. And, more importantly perhaps, it makes things a lot cheaper.

So I knew that Eamon would supply the goods when I asked him to.

Someone would soon be getting a lot of grief. I was actually looking forward to it. My weird sense of humour. I just hoped it didn't get me into too much trouble this time.

Apart from one other little job I had to do, I was about ready. I decided it was time to see where the enemy, aka Albert Collins lived.

Depending on where and how you lived the evening meal got called differently. In our house it was always Tea. The lunch time meal was dinner. Tonight Lynne was doing the cooking.

She does this now and then. Normally I do the cooking because, well, because I am a better cook.

Some of the roadkill stews I used to cook up in my truck were to die for. One guy nearly did. He must have had a delicate stomach or something.

But tonight, The Boss was cooking. Something healthy, trendy and probably unpronounceable.

After a suitable wait, I was called for my tea. It was egg and chips. Not complaining but not what I expected. I sneaked a look in the green compost bin later. Another culinary failure.

But, give her some due, she does try. A lot of people say that she is very trying.

Dunchurch is only ten minutes from our house and I quickly found the street I wanted. Moot Lane was a fairly quiet with a row of around 30 houses. I soon spotted the house I wanted. The front garden was immaculate in comparison to others in the street. Obviously the same compulsion for perfection wasn't restricted to just the allotment.

If the guy wasn't such an obvious bully, blackmailer and all round bastard it would have been admirable.

There was a white van in the driveway and I quickly memorized the registration. Just to be sure, I took a quick photo with the Nikon digital camera I always carry.

It used to be part of my journalist kit and I liked having it in the car. You never know when you might need pictures for insurance purposes.

I drove away before becoming to conspicuous. I was using my Landcruiser so I didn't think Collins would recognize me as he hadn't seen me in it before. I normally had it garaged when not using it.

But, once Eamon had delivered the goods, I would have to park it outside.

Eamon's delivery would have to go in the garage out of sight until I had finished with it.

Hopefully, that wouldn't be too long. That however, depended on the local police.

15: The Allotment!

If there was one thing Collins really liked it was people being afraid of him. Even as a young boy there was something about him that made people wary and afraid.

Now, here at the allotment, he could sense that fear. People looked at him when they thought he couldn't see them. Those he talked to never quite looked him squarely in the face. He guessed the news of the burnt shed had already become hot gossip.

Of course, he sympathised and tut-tutted along with everyone else. But, inwardly, he glowed every time he saw the heap of burnt tools outside the main gate. He saw the remains of the shed on the skip and it was all he could do not to burst out laughing.

But, he was sure that wouldn't be the end of it. The newcomer, that so called co-worker of that stuck up Geoff, didn't look like the type to give in easily.

He could still remember the fear and panic that had set in when he couldn't break the other's grip. What business of his was it to stick his nose in when he was showing Geoff not to cross him?

Even now he could feel the burn of humiliation as the newcomer forced him to the ground and then made him apologise. Even worse was the apparent ease with which he achieved it. He hadn't even broken into a sweat. No-one had done that to him for a very long time.

No doubt it was the talk of the allotment by now. Well, that was soon to change. The shed was just the start. From now on, he was going to do all that he could to get rid of Geoff and his new best mate.

Just then he heard laughter. Looking up towards the Top end, he saw a group of men pointing at something. He followed the direction of their gaze and saw five men walking down the path from the back gate end.

As they got nearer, he could see that it was the newcomer, Big Mick, Paul, Adrian and Pete. For some reason they were all wearing red baseball caps. And, as they got even nearer, he saw red braces and what looked like cushions stuffed under their shirts.

Even more curiously, they were all walking in a funny way. A sort of a straight back, rolling walk that seemed somehow familiar. Every one of them had a scowl on his face.

As they passed him, they looked straight ahead and continued past his plots and towards the far end.

Even as he put some tools way, he watched them continue on a complete circuit of the allotments. What the hell was all that about?

He saw Little Mick coming towards him. Obviously the little runt was finished and was going home. He beckoned him over. "What's going on? What were those pratts doing?"

The older man looked around nervously. He moistened his lips, his eyes darting about. Finally, he looked up. "They were taking the mickey. Didn't you get it?"

"Get what? Who were they taking the mickey out of?"

Little Mick swallowed, tried to get some moisture into a suddenly dry mouth. Finally, in a small hoarse voice, he managed to reply.

"You" he blurted out. "They were taking the mickey out of you. Didn't you see the red baseball caps, the braces and the way they were walking?" Even as he was talking, Little Mick was edging towards the gate and freedom.

He was right to be afraid. Suddenly, Collins' face went dark red as he finally realised the truth of what he had just been told.

They were taking the mickey out of him? Four doddery pensioners and a fat bastard? With the whole allotment looking on and laughing? Well, he vowed to himself, they weren't going to get away with that.

They wanted a war, they had got it. They had started it but he would finish it.

16: The Allotment!

Big Mick had barely got to the end of the path when he burst out laughing. "Did you see his face? He had no idea what was going on."

Pete pointed towards the gate. "He will have now. His little grass is telling him. Look."

Sure enough, we saw Little Mick talking to Collins.

"He won't like that. He doesn't like people making fun of him." Adrian said with a smile twitching.

We did look funny. All with red baseball hats, braces and those little cushions shoved up our fronts. As we walked round the allotment, most of the people quickly got what we were doing. Keeping a straight face as we marched past Collins was the hard part. Now it was just wait and see time. The general consensus was that there would be consequences.

Which was where the rest of my plan came in.

I had phoned my mate Eamon this morning, given him the registration of Collins van from last night's photo and was told to expect my delivery around mid-day.

I had then phoned Adrian and asked him to contact the others and meet me by the back gate. Adrian had managed two red caps and one set of red braces. Pete delivered two pairs of braces, one black, one brown.

Big Mick brought nothing whilst Paul had one set of braces. I ended up with a spare set of braces and two red caps after making up the deficiencies. Plus the five little cushions I had bought in yesterday's charity shop trawl. A modest outlay but one that I hoped would be worth it. We had dressed ourselves by the gate and then began our march.

For the rest of the time we were on the plots we wore our Collins gear. Every now and then someone would go past and have a little laugh.

There wasn't really much to do on the plots at this time of the year. September is a bit of a lull after the summer crop of fruit had all been picked. The remaining vegetables were used on an as and when basis. Mainly it was just tidying up.

Following our agreement, everyone put their best tools in Adrian's garage for safe keeping. We expected there would be repercussions as we continued our strategy and we wanted to limit any damage to the bare minimum.

The others agreed that their ramshackle sheds weren't worth worrying about and were prepared to sacrifice them for the cause. Other than the sheds and a few crops there wasn't much else to be damaged once the tools were removed.

We had also agreed who was likely to experience the first attack. It would be the one who provoked Collins the most.

Paul's shed was the most dilapidated so he volunteered to annoy our target the most in the hope that he would be retaliated on first. Which is where the other item from my home came in.

What I was looking for in my house shed, aka The Command Centre, was what is called a trail camera. Basically a battery powered camera housed in a secure box and triggered by an infra red beam. You have probably seen them on nature and wildlife programmes.

They are set up in remote locations and record anything, man or beast, that wandered into their field of view and the infra red beam.

As they also work well in darkness they have proved invaluable in recording rare and endangered nocturnal animals. They are relatively small in size and, unless you are specifically looking, not easily spotted.

I intended to set my camera up so it kept watch on Paul's shed. That way, night or day –but probably mostly under cover of darkness – there would be a date and time stamped record of the vandalism that we expected.

The plan was that Paul would go out of his way to annoy Collins so he would be the first victim of his revenge. But, to be on the safe side, the camera also recorded the main path as well. I would come back later this evening and set it up.

There would probably be a lot of recordings of the other plot holders going about their legitimate business but it didn't really matter.

The lithium batteries that powered the camera would last a long time. And the sd card that the images recorded onto would automatically delete and re-record when full.

Basically I only had to look at the recordings once something had happened. I didn't think Collins would do anything quite so soon after Geoff's shed but we fully intended to provoke a response. And to get the record of that response recorded indisputably on my trail camera.

The other part of my plan was to cost Collins a lot of money. I hadn't told the others about this side of it because I didn't want them involved in anything as illegal as what I was about to do.

Nor, being a loner and cautious as well, did I want to rely too much on the others keeping their mouths shut.

16: The Allotment!

Eamon delivered on time. He rolled up in his beat up car transporter and parked outside my garage. I had already parked my vehicle on the road and left the garage door open.

Within a matter of minutes a white Vauxhall van was off his truck and into the garage. I quickly shut the doors and hoped there weren't too many nosy neighbours about.

Eamon didn't want to stop for a cuppa as he was in a hurry.

"Thanks, mate, I owe you one. Couple of weeks ok?"

"Yes, you do." He reminded me. "No hurry and I don't want it traced back to me. The reg plates are inside. Call me when you are finished. And, no, I don't want to know."

Eamon was a good bloke to know. Mind you, he probably said exactly the same about me. Contacts and favours. The fuel of life.

Before I used the van, I had a couple of things to do to it. First I had to black the back windows out. That reminded me I had to go onto Ebay. I also had to change the registration plates over.

I already had some black window tint in my man cave from a previous vehicle. All I need now was a couple of stickers. I had zoomed in on my photo of Collins vehicle and was able to see the two stickers on the back windows more clearly. I guessed I would be able find similar items on Ebay.

As it turned out I was right. A few minutes on-line and two identical *No tools left in this vehicle overnight* stickers were ordered with delivery expected in 2-3 days.

I decided to wait until they had arrived and do all three little jobs in one go.

Then I would have a white van that looked more or less identical to that driven by Mr Albert Collins.

Then the fun would start. Well, more accurately, the fun would start about a fortnight after I used my white van. Expensive fun, I hoped. And, not my expense either.

In the meantime I had some phoning to do. I phoned the town hall. I was put through very efficiently to the office of John Burns, the deputy manager of Parks and Recreation. I was told he was out of the office and could I leave a message? Instead I asked for, and was given, his email address. That would do just as well. And, if my suspicions were right, probably better.

Dear Mr Burns, I would like to arrange a meeting to discuss the situation on the Victory Allotments.

One tenant is making threats and causing damage to the plots of other tenants. I had imagined that the Council's response would be to investigate such accusations.

However, from speaking to other tenants, I find little evidence to support this.

Does Rugby Borough Council actively support vandalism and threats towards the tenants of its allotment? You may be aware that my co-worker's shed was burnt down recently and this was not the first shed to be destroyed.

Therefore I would like a meeting with you at your earliest convenience to discuss this matter further and to hear your response. You can contact me via email or my house landline number which you will have on record.

Otherwise I shall be obliged to report this matter to the police and to inform both of the local papers of the situation at these allotments and the council's response or lack of it. Regards Dave Williams

Now that I had made it official, he would have to respond. Failing this, I would be within my rights to take it further up the command chain.

And, if the rumors were true, he would also discuss it with Collins.

*****

Down on the allotment, Collins heard his phone ringing. He walked over to his shed and fished it out of his coat pocket. He checked the ID. What did that pratt want?

"Bert? It's John Burns. Listen I've just received an email from that new guy, Dave Williams? You know, the posh bloke's co-worker. He's making allegations about the allotments and threatening to go to the police and the local papers."

"What do you mean making allegations? What is he saying? And, is he accusing me?"

"Well, no. Not directly. But he wants a meeting to discuss the threats and vandalism going on. He mentioned a shed burnt recently. Was that you?"

"Listen, you little turd. Don't even ask that question again. Stall for as long as you can. I'll handle him."

"I'm not so sure you can. He seems very determined. If I don't have a meeting with him, he could go over my head. And, if he goes to the police, it will be official and out of my hands. I can't risk my job."

"I said, I'll handle it. And remember, you only have a job as long as I keep quiet. Williams will see the light. I'll make sure of that."

Collins put the phone back. Typical of Burns. Coming crying to him at the first sign of trouble.

He looked around the allotments. Up on the Top end he saw Adrian Miles on his patch. His white hair made identification easy. He put his tools back, shut his shed and walked up the path.

As he got nearer, he called out "Oi, I want a word with you."

He had a satisfied grin on his face as he noted the other's discomfort. Scared, just like he liked them.

"Tell your mate Dave that I am not scared of him. He got lucky the last time. He won't be the next time. Tell him that if he goes to the police or papers, he'll regret it. Got that?" He waited until the other nodded his head. Satisfied, he went back. Made sure his sheds were secure and left. He'd come back later after dark and make sure the old guy got the message loud and clear.

*****

I was pottering around in the back garden. I had got pottering down to a fine art. I looked busy but wasn't really doing much.

Lynne called out that I had a visitor. Adrian with the white hair came up the path. What was it about his hair colour that women went all mushy over?

"Got a minute?" he asked.

I motioned him into my shed. "What's up" I asked as he went in.

"I've just been threatened by Collins. He sends a message. I don't know what it means but he says you'll regret it if you go to the police or papers. He also said he's not scared of you. That you got lucky the last time and won't be the next time. Does it make sense to you."

"Yes, it does. Did he actually say the police and papers? "

Adrian nodded.

"Good, that didn't take long." I told him about the email I had sent to John Burns less than an hour ago. He seemed a bit puzzled. "What about it?"

"Don't you see? It means that Burns has been in touch with Collins after he read my email."

" I imagine that you thought he would. Are you surprised or what?"

"You're not thinking this through. I send Burns an email, a private email, and he discusses it with someone else less than an hour later. Someone who is not a council employee."

Adrian's face lit up as the penny dropped. " A confidential email that is covered by the Data Protection Act or something? He tells Collins and then I get told to tell you. He won't be able to wriggle out of that one so easily."

"Right, you are my witness. Collins definitely said police and papers. That was in the email. So how did he know that if he hadn't been told? So now I can get to see Burns. He won't be able to refuse to see me now. If he does then I have enough to get him into a lot of trouble with his boss."

"Right, nice one. And, as I am a witness, maybe I ought to come with you when you meet Burns. I can tell him a lot of other things as well."

I was just about to agree when the staff came up the path. "That posh bloke from over the road is here. Wants a word if you are not busy."

I thanked her –always pays to be polite to staff. Especially those who prepare your meals and drinks – and let her get on with her duties. Probably an afternoon of computer games and Facethingy or Twatter. She smiled warmly at Adrian and left.

Ol' White Hair and I eventually found Geoff at the front door. He was in his best I'm Important suit and tie. He looked a bit annoyed as if not used to being kept waiting. His mood didn't lighten when he saw Adrian either. I guess it would be a private word then.

I told Adrian I would see him later. He took the hint and left.

"Hello, Geoff. What can I do for you?"

"It's Geoffrey" he said automatically. "What was he doing here?"

"Just came to ask my advice on which spuds to plant next year."

"Oh, allotment stuff. Good, because that's why I am here." He paused, then in a rush, " I'm giving up the allotment. Would you like to carry on with it?"

Excellent news. "But why, Geoffrey? You have put so much into it. Don't let Collins run you off. If you do then he has won."

"Surprisingly it has nothing to do with Collins or the allotment for that matter. It's just that the wife and I have had a long chat and decided it is best to part company."

"Oh, sorry to hear that. How do you feel about it? Sad, annoyed glad?"

He cleared his throat. "Actually, I was pleased. My wife is quite content living her own life and doesn't want to move. I have just been promoted to run my own branch in Luton. It is a bit far to commute easily so I would have had to move anyway."

"How does your wife feel about that?" I asked.

"That is what prompted the conversation initially and, suddenly, everything just came out. My wife is neither sad or glad. She agrees that it is time for moving on provided that everything is kept private.

We'll get a divorce and she can keep the house and will get a good allowance. Jane is leaving her husband and moving down to Luton with me. The promotion is a big step up for me and I couldn't turn it down.

Now, surprisingly, everything has worked out really well. And, if you want to take on the plot, then it has worked for you as well."

"Wow. Well, Geoffrey, I am genuinely pleased for you. That must be a big weight off your shoulders?"

Actually he did seem different. Still hopelessly up himself but slightly more relaxed and, though perhaps not quite a smile, with a slightly less haughty expression. "You won't believe how much. Suddenly everything is clear cut and sorted." He almost blurted out.

"I can actually look forward and finalize things now instead of sneaking around with the expectation of being found out. It's like my life has just started again."

Almost automatically I held out my hand and we shook. We didn't do the Man Hug thing. Geoff hadn't changed that much.

"I'll write a letter to the council explaining about my promotion and giving up the allotment. I'll recommend that you be allowed to keep it. I'll get it in the post today."

Oh-Oh. I didn't want John Burns to know about this until after our meeting. No point in giving him any ammunition or leverage.

"Er, actually Geoffrey I have a meeting with John Burns tomorrow." I lied as I thought furiously. "It's about getting the council to hold an allotment competition to generate some *espirit de corps* and inter – allotment rivalry. If you could drop it through my letterbox, I could give it to him personally. I'll tell him you asked me to give it to him personally and to thank him for his help."

He considered this. Nodded his head. "An interesting thought about a competition. You are really getting into this allotment business aren't you?"

I nodded my head furiously and held my breath.

"Yes, I agree with you, it would be more personal and professional as well. Ok, I'll get it written and drop it in an envelope. I'll probably drop it off later this evening. I won't knock. I'll just pop it through."

"Thank you Geoffrey. That will be fine. Now, may I wish you every success and happiness in your new life? It couldn't have happened to a more deserving person." *Steady, I reminded myself. Tone down the sarcasm.*

He nodded his head in obvious agreement. Decided that there was nothing more to add and walked off. There was definitely more spring in his step. I was glad he was getting his life sorted. Everyone deserved a little happiness now and again.

Maybe I should follow his example? Naw, on second thoughts she would kill me. I could think about getting my hair dyed white though. Might earn me a few brownie points.

17: The Allotment!

There was an email from John Burns in my box the very next morning. Short and sweet. Asking if 11 am would be convenient for me as this was the only available slot in a busy schedule.

Rugby Town Hall is a big building on the edge of Caldecott Park. It was built in the post war modernisation period.

Just a brick slab of a place with pretentious pillars and wide steps leading through the front door. Inside it is as bland and uninspiring as any other similar building.

I asked at reception and a few minutes later a young lady came to escort me to John Burn's office. It too turned out to be an uninspiring place within another. A couple of prints were on the off white/cream coloured walls. A desk, two chairs, a sliver of carpet and that was that.

The view from the window showed the easily forgettable Cemex Cement headquarters. It used to be Rugby Cement but was sold to the world wide corporation some years back. I was looking out the window when John Burns entered.

He was a early 30's, tall and thin guy. Good head of hair – you notice these things when your forehead keeps getting bigger and bigger – and a worried expression beneath it.

He gestured to the seat opposite the desk. I held out my hand but he choose to ignore it. Ok, two can play at that game. I waited until he had sat down and remained standing.

"My back is playing up a bit. It's a bit uncomfortable sitting down." I explained from my position of authority. I could see he didn't like being seated whilst I stood. But, other than standing himself, he couldn't do much about it.

"I got your email." He said unnecessarily. Of course he had. Why else would I be here? "What's it all about? You mentioned something about threats and vandalism?"

He was worried. His eyes were all over the place and his forehead had a sweat sheen to it. His hands were busy fussing on his desk. Moving things about unnecessarily.

I decided it was better the cut straight to the chase. "You know exactly what it is about. You have obviously discussed it with Bert Collins. Otherwise how could he know the contents of the email I sent you? He sent me a threat via another plot holder. Saying that if I went to the police or the press, I would regret it."

His mouth opened but not much came out. His eyes darted here and there, seeking escape. Finally "I don't know what you are talking about." He said in a hoarse voice.

"Well, ok then. If that is the case then I will have to go above your head. Someone in this department is leaking what is supposed to be confidential information to someone other than a council employee. Even without the threats to me, that is a serious offence. You know, Data Protection Act and all that? Someone could lose their job and be prosecuted over that." I turned and made to walk out the door.

I almost made it before he broke. "Wait, can we discuss this?" I tried to keep the smile off my face. For one moment there I thought my bluff had been called.

I walked back and stood at his side. Looking down from a commanding position. He put his head in his hands and, almost in a whisper, asked "What do you want?"

Most of what I knew about interviews, interrogation and otherwise obtaining information came from books, film and tv. During my years as a journalist I had found most of the stuff I had read or watched usually worked.

I had since fine-tuned it on the job, as it were. Over the last few years I had interviewed truck drivers, transport managers, fitters and others involved in the lower end of transport.

At the top end I had interviewed CEO's of large organisations. Getting information had been part of my job and I had been good at it.

The most effective thing was silence. I would ask a question and then wait. When the interviewee spoke, ask another question quickly. Get a rhythm going Pretty soon the answers would come with little hesitation and virtually no think time. No time to withhold some aspects of an operation, projected growth, expected income or similar.

It was also useful to build up a rapport. Get my likeability factor going. Get everyone relaxed.

"First of all John…. I can call you John, can I? Let me first tell you that I am not a journalist anymore." Quickly establishing that I had been a journalist and would, presumably, still have connections.

He nodded. Whether to being called "John" or my employment status. He looked up at me and repeated the question.

"What sort of hold does Collins have over you? It must be something pretty good for you to protect him like this." He started to protest but I cut him off.

"Too late for that now, John. There is something or I wouldn't still be here. I have nothing personally against you. I have only just met you. But the allotment gossip is that Collins has something on you." He started to shake his head.

"Now, are you going to tell me the whole story and maybe we can work together or…..well, you know the alternative." He swallowed and then, in almost a whisper, he confessed his secret.

"I've…. I've been having an affair with one of the girls in the Treasury department. We thought we had been careful but Collins spotted us together one evening. He obviously followed us and took some pictures of us…..doing…. having…. You know?"

I patted his shoulder for reassurance. "Having sex, you mean. That's no real biggie is it? What's the worst that could happen? You get a divorce, get forgiven or get fired?"

He shook his head. "You don't understand. My wife is older than me and has money from her late husband. My salary alone couldn't keep us in our current lifestyle.

So, not only would I lose my home and all the perks but my job as well. The head of the council is a relative of hers."

"But, you could always get another job, right? Move away with your lady friend. One of my friends in a similar situation came round last night and told me almost exactly the same thing. He got it sorted with his wife and is moving away with his girl friend. You're young enough to do the same surely?" I asked.

"I don't really want to. It is just a sex thing. My wife is older and is pretty past that sort of thing. And I only got this job because her relative overlooked the fact that I have a conviction for fraud. One word from her and I am out of both my home and my job."

His face fell and, for a moment, I thought he would start to cry. "Have you any idea how difficult it is in today's climate to get a good job when you have a record? Particularly one for Fraud and Deception. Just a few petrol receipts but a conviction and police record just the same"

"So, that's it. That is the hold Collins has. The Affair? I take it he found out about the conviction as well?" Burns nodded, wiped his eyes.

" That is why he can do pretty much what he wants down the allotments?" I needed him to say it.

"Yes….. I keep getting complaints but ignore them or try to soothe them over. I have offered him another allotment somewhere else but he wants to stay where he is.

Not that it makes difference in the long run. The Council has already earmarked the Victory Allotments as a potential site for new homes. It will make more money with new houses than with an allotment. So, what are you going to do? Tell my boss?"

Well, that was a bit of a blow about the allotments being sold off. As to the other, well if Collins lost his support from Burns, that made getting rid of him easier, didn't it?

In the end, it was left that I would keep my mouth shut provided he gave no further support to Collins.

If fact, I told him to distance himself as far as he could because the manure was about to start hitting the fan. And fast.

I also told him that I would be asking for his help in getting rid of his former problem. I would be back when I knew exactly what I wanted. And, that I expected his fullest co-operation.

In the meantime, if Collins tried anything else, I was to be told. Not surprisingly he was very eager to help now. Before he had seen no way out, now….well, maybe, just maybe, there was someone shining a light at the end of the tunnel.

At best he had a chance. At worst, the same problem as before.

"Oh, John. There is something else." I handed over Geoff's letter of resignation and request that I be allowed to carry on the allotment. He picked it up and read through it.

"That won't be as problem will it?" I asked. "And, before you start to think that you have exchanged one blackmailer for another, there are no strings attached. You either say I get it or I don't."

He obviously had been thinking just that. Suddenly, he smiled up at me. "I don't think there will be any problems. You are just the type of person we want down there. Consider it done. I'll drop you an official line to confirm it."

This time he stood up, held out his hand and we shook. It might have been my imagination but, suddenly, he seemed taller, younger and more confident.

As I walked out of the Town Hall, I felt a bit better as well. What could have been a tough problem had turned out to be easy.

I was also struck by how alike Geoff and Burn's problems were. Both seeing a younger woman. Both married to older woman who didn't seem interested in sex anymore. And both being blackmailed by Collins.

Personally I could never understand the attraction, the deep seated need to always be seeking complicated sex.

I knew lots of guys who never turned anything down whether the person involved was single, married or spoken for.

Most of those guys were divorced, living on their own and shelling out the bulk of their money in maintenance.

I could never understand why they risked everything for a quickie. If things weren't going well at home then get it sorted or get out.

One old guy once told me that sex was like having a car.

When you first got a new or second hand car, it was different, better equipped, faster or whatever than what you had before.

Get a few miles under it's belt and it became normal and routine. You tended to take it's comforts, reliability and bodywork for granted.

Once you got bored with that car, you traded up and experienced the same excitement you first had with your old car. But, once again, a little further down the road, things once again became boring.

I think the point he was trying to make is that sex with anyone is still basically the same. Same basic function. Trade up and it's still the same. Far better to keep your old model, look after it and appreciate it.

I've had my old banger a few years now. And, I still appreciate her reliability, comfort and bodywork.

18: The Allotment!

I spent most of the afternoon preparing my van. I put the dark tint film on the back windows and then the recently arrived stickers. I changed the number plates and my work was nearly done. Except for one tiny detail.

I was sure I had it stowed away in my workshop. I tend to keep things, like most older men. You never know when you might need that screw, tiny bit of wood or broken tool. Best keep it, just in case, was my motto. I eventually found what I was looking for not too far from where I thought it had been.

As I fixed the large red poppy to the van grill, I knew it had been worth the effort. It was all in the detail.

Victory Drive is a mix of single and dual carriageways. Coming from the town centre it is mostly single then, just up the road from our house, it becomes dual carriageway.

The single lane section is notorious for its many speed bumps. These slow vehicles down, as intended but, once onto the dual section, most vehicles speed up to make up the lost time. And, as the first dual section is mostly downhill, the legal speed limit is quickly reached and exceeded.

To counteract this flagrant breach of traffic regulations, the police frequently set up mobile speed camera units.

That these cameras, on this particular stretch of road at least, are very profitable, is purely co-incidental.

The impatient motorist hits the dual carriageway section and almost instantly gooses the go pedal.

And, because this road is one of the best ways to get to the sprawling warehouse complex at DIRFT it carries a lot of traffic at starting and knocking off times. Throw in the school run and it gets busy at peak times.

Add a blind bend at each end where single becomes dual and you have motorists speeding straight into the lens of the strategically placed waiting speed camera.

Locals tend not to get caught out but other drivers are in frame before they even straighten out from the bend and register that the camera is there. So, a nice little earner for the police and safer roads for us.

Except, of course, at night time when the reckless youths race up and down with their cars. You probably have them down your road as well

Souped up buzz boxes with rubber band tyres and dramatically lowered suspension using the road as a race track.

Usually accompanied, of course, by the growl from an exhaust pipe that looks like it is on Viagra and an ear bending and monotonous BOOM BOOM through slightly open blacked out windows.

But, for me the main attraction of this speed camera is that it is on the route that Collins uses daily to get to and from his allotment.

Add in several other fixed and mobile cameras on his route to and from Dunchurch and there is a lot of potential for his white van, with the blacked out rear windows, to be caught speeding.

Not just on his daily route either. There are lots of speed cameras on the busy A45 trunk road that runs through Dunchurch to Coventry and on to Birmingham.

Not that I was going to be out and out speeding. Just a few mph over the speed limit is enough for a speeding ticket. I intended to have a few runs up and down my road when the camera was operating. The fixed units I could trigger at night when the traffic and roads were lighter.

Basically an identical white van with the same registration plates would be collecting a lot of speeding fines over the next week.

I very much doubted that I would be identified as the driver with a baseball hat pulled down low.

Sneaky? Out of order? Morally reprehensible? Illegal? Probably. But still a good idea.

The chances of me being pulled over for driving a vehicle with false plate were low. All I had to do was drive legally until my sat nav warned me that a speed camera was operating. Then I would speed up an extra 15mph or so and get captured.

I could easily picture the scene when a bewildered Collins would be swamped under a deluge of speeding tickets. Lets see him argue his way out of that lot.

Did I feel sorry for the guy? Not really. He started it. He threatened, blackmailed and destroyed. We would finish it. He wanted us out. We wanted him out and for peace to return the allotments. I reckon that came under the Fair Means or Foul trade description.

Of course, note that I said "we". So far it was "me" and a lot of talk from the "We" section. That was going to change as well.

With the other members of the so called "One for All and All for One" Allotmenteers personally involved, silence would indeed be golden.

But, for the moment, my white van driving was going to be my guilty secret and mine alone.

19: The Allotment!

Strangely, John Burns felt relieved. He had been dreading his secret coming out almost as much as he had hated being bulled by Collins.

He was even contemplating confessing and accepting the consequences. The affair was finished: both knew that in their hearts.

Whether his wife would be forgiving would be another matter. Maybe it would be the sort of thing she wouldn't want becoming public knowledge. There was only one way to find out.

And, if she did lash out and things turned nasty, what could she do? Would it matter if he lost his job? Or his home? Probably not. He was still young enough to start over. Of course there was still the conviction hanging over his head but not all jobs required voluntary disclosure of criminal convictions.

With his work experience he could go anywhere to work. Probably.

No matter how it ended, it would end today. No more blackmailing. Just accept the consequences and move on.

*****

Albert Collins was having a break. He was in his large shed and drinking tea from a flask. He had been on his second allotment looking for signs of disturbance. He didn't find any but he was still uneasy.

He had suddenly realised that he wasn't going to have things his own way this time. That new bloke had somehow stirred up the others into uniting against him.

Making fun of him for all the others to see. Well, they would all pay for that. If he was careful there would be no comeback. Oh sure, they might suspect but suspecting and proving was different.

One thing was certain, he wasn't going anywhere voluntarily. Not this time. There would be no repeat of the humiliation he suffered on his last allotment. Walking up to the gate and finding all his stuff thrown out was bad enough.

Having his shed dismantled and stacked against the railings was the ultimate humiliation. It couldn't happen again. He couldn't afford to let it happen a second time.

He was going to have to lean on John Burns to get a couple of people thrown off. Once that had happened he could regain control again.

Get the allotments up and running again. Become productive with every plot taken. With people he had picked and could control.

Once that had happened, the council would have to think twice about selling his allotments for building plots. That wouldn't, couldn't, happen. Not in his lifetime.

After that, well, it wouldn't matter anyway.

They wanted a fight? Bring it on.

*****

Adrian Miles looked over the allotments from his kitchen window. It was a view he never got tired of. There was always something different to see with the seasons. The stark beauty of the plots in winter. The bustle of the plot holders getting ready for Spring. Cultivating, planting, weeding and waiting.

Waiting for his favourite season: the long summer weeks. The weeks when everywhere was a riot of colour and productivity. When the backbreaking Spring preparation began to thrust its rewards up through the productive soil.

The gentle months through to autumn. The tidying, whether the harvest was good or not, just being at one with the earth. The sowing, the tending, the weeding, the picking, preparing and the eating. The endless cycle of nature.

He appreciated it even more the last couple of years. The void since his wife had died of the malignant growth that had slowly robbed her of her mind, her dignity and, eventually, her will to go on.

During those long dark days it was only the hard labour and the distracting hours on the allotment that had kept him going.

Kept him from listening to the dark voices that whispered in his ear. That told him how easy it would be. How they would be together again.

It had taken time but he was getting there. Getting used to being a single unit when he had spent most of his life as a team.

The allotments had saved his sanity. Of that there was no doubt. Now it was his turn to save the allotments from Collins….if he could.

Somehow, the new guy's arrival had provided the catalyst some of them had been looking for. The will to unite against a common enemy. To prevail as good over evil.

To get the allotments back to what it had once been. A haven of tranquility in a world that was gradually getting more and more alien for him and others like him.

The Allotmenteers –strange how that silly name had caught on and become a symbol – would do their best to regain that lost peace.

Even though, as history had shown, peace usually came at a price. Generally, there had to be a war before there could be peace.

And, he at least, was prepared to dig deep to pay that price. He hoped the others could, would, do the same.

Mick, "Big Mick, McAvoy was indulging in his favourite pastime. He was in the ramshackle, tin, wood, nail and hope creation that he optimistically called a shed.

He was sitting on an old plastic chair that had been thrown for the bin men. He wasn't concerned about appearances, just functionality. Right now the old shed and the old chair were allowing him to indulge in his old vice.

Slowly, almost reverently, he reached into the paper bag and extracted one of the three Greggs sausage rolls it contained.

He had bought them before coming on to the allotment. It had become almost a daily ritual. If not sausage rolls, then a couple of pies. To be consumed in the sanctuary of his shed without his wife's constant nagging about his weight.

Ok, he conceded, maybe he could lose a couple of pounds. It was getting harder and harder to get into the cab of his vehicle. Not just getting in but fitting in. He could almost believe that he had a permanent groove in his belly from the steering wheel.

But he was getting older. And people always put on weight when they got older, didn't they? He would be 36 on his next birthday. Of course he would put on a bit of weight.

That had been the whole point of getting the allotment he suddenly remembered. His wife's insistence on exercise and the health aspects of eating vegetables grown on said allotment.

Did the health aspect count if he only ate his Greggs' stuff on the allotment, he wondered idly as he picked up his second ambrosial offering.

Not that there had been many vegetables taken home for consumption. He had planted too late, hadn't weeded, watered, cared or cossetted them enough if he was honest.

But he still liked being down here. Apart from his secret eating, he appreciated the peace and the company of the other guys.

Mind you, if the Allotmenteers had anything to do with it, that peace looked likely to be shattered soon.

The Allotmenteers. One for All and All for One. He liked the concept of it. That new guy was pretty clever coming up with a name like that.

Of course, it had generally been agreed that Collins couldn't be allowed to go on with his bullying. But now it looked like something positive was finally being done. And, best of all, he was part of it.

Ok, up to now all they had done was dress up like Collins and wind him up. His face had been a treat once he realised what was going on.

But now there was talk of something more positive. Of actually provoking Collins to lash out. If it meant sacrificing his shed for the cause, then so be it.

That was what being an Allotmenteer was all about. One for All and All for One.

Plus they had to meet in a pub for all that planning. That was no hardship either.

He would miss his shed though, he realised as he savoured the last sausage roll. Maybe Paul's shed would do instead?

*****

Paul Tiler leant on his fork. He had ben digging for some time now and had worked up a good sweat. He took his handkerchief out of his pants pocket, removed his cap and swabbed it over his bald pate. There was a definite demarcation line between his tan face and white forehead.

He had seen Big Mick going into his shed earlier. Carrying a Greggs bag as usual, he had noted.

That guy was a heart attack waiting to happen. Drank like a fish too, as had been noted the other night at the pub.

Idly he wondered just why the big guy had an allotment in the first place. He never seemed to do anything with it.

Almost automatically, he carried on digging. Fork in, lean back, pick up, turn the earth, replace and onto the next forkful. Positive work that you could see the results of.

Good exercise and a way of saving money on vegetables. Neither he or his wife were big eaters so there was always a lot of produce over to be sold to neighbours.

Sometimes he wondered if he ought to put in for another plot. Double his output and maybe his earnings. He had thought about it for sometime now and discarded the idea because there were no vacant plots near this one.

He had thought about teaming up with Big Mick but quickly realised he would be doing all the work for half the produce. No sense in that. Might as well get his own second plot and get all the benefits.

He could have a word with old Albert of course. The word was that he was retiring. That he had lost heart after the arson that had destroyed all his raspberry bushes.

Of course there were some good vacant plots on the Lower End. But that meant moving into Collins' territory and he didn't want to do that. Not until he had gone anyway. And who knew when, or if, that was going to happen?

Again he wondered about the mad impulse that had made him join the new guy's group. What had Big Mick called it? The Allotmenteers?

But, what if they did succeed? Got rid of Collins. There would be nothing to stop him having another plot then. With Collins gone the whole atmosphere of the allotments would change overnight.

The tangible Them and Us feeling which the bastard had instigated would go. It would be like the post war Peace had come to the allotments again.

Paul Tiler removed his cap once again. Wiped, replaced and forked. Sod it, he was going to do his best to get rid of that blight on all their lives.

If it cost him a shed then that was a small price. One he would be glad to pay. "Yes", he thought, as he turned over the rich dark soil "Yes, I am in."

*****

Slowly Pete Wills turned the handle on his lathe. He was in his double garage which served as his workshop as well. He was making a new throttle control rod for his old steam engine.

Not a full size one –although he would have loved one – but the one he had been given as a 10 year old.

Sold as a toy, it did, however, possess all the scaled down working details and capabilities of the larger machine it was based on.

Now, he was refurbishing it. Making it as good as new for his older grandson. The only one so far to show any sign of inheriting his passion for engineering.

Must have skipped a generation, he mused, as he shaved an almost miniscule amount off the steel rod. Another few hours and the steam engine would be finished.

Just finish this control rod and then down to the allotments to get a few onions, carrots, spuds and a cabbage for tomorrow's dinner, he thought.

Time was, he used to go down the allotments for the peace and tranquility it offered. Now he preferred his garage. Things were getting far from peaceful down there now. Idly he wondered what damage he would find when he did go down.

So far, most of the Top plots had escaped the Wrath of Collins as he termed it in film ideology.

The posh bloke's shed and old Bert's raspberry bushes. It hadn't taken much for the posh bloke to move on. Not that he was much of a loss. Hardly spoke and spent most of the time in his passion palace with his bit of skirt.

He had been pleased when Dave had told him the news about taking over permanently. He was interesting to speak to and a good worker too. Good eye for detail. Would have made a good engineer.

But, when Dave started talking about all the places he had taken a truck to, his engineering career seemed pretty tame. And those trucks were really incredible pieces of engineering as well.

Bit late now but it was a job that he thought he would have enjoyed.

Mind, some of the stories Dave told were pretty hair raising. Enough to make you realise it wasn't a job just anyone could handle.

.Sleeping with a knife under his pillow. Fighting off hijackers on the way to Saudi Arabia. Makeshift repairs that demonstrated good basic engineering. A "just get on with it" attitude that most jobs didn't provide.

But, most of all, it was the guy's quiet confidence, that came across. The confidence that suggested, no matter what was thrown at him, he could cope, would get it sorted.

When Adrian had told him of how quickly and efficiently he had dealt with Collins he didn't quite believe it.

But, having spent some time with him, it was obvious that he didn't perceive the Collins' of the world as a threat. More as something to deal with and move on. Just the type of guy the allotment people needed to have on their side.

So, yes, he had no doubt that things were finally coming to a head on the allotments. Maybe they would go back to how they were before Collins moved in five years ago.

When people helped each other and there was no Top Or Lower factions. No intentional arson, plot damage, intimidation or looking over your shoulder before voicing an opinion.

In truth, he was quite looking forward to it. He had already carried out the task that Dave had asked of him yesterday. One that suited his special talents.

He had waited until Collins had moved down the Top allotments to speak with little Mick.

Without being too obvious, he had wheeled a barrow full of rubbish down to the main gate and the big council skip.

Once out of sight, he had gone to the white Vauxhall van and quickly picked the lock on the fuel filler cap.

He only used two of his slim pieces of metal or picks. First he slid the L shaped Tension Wrench into the cylinder. This opened up the lock to allow the Slim Pick access.

Using this custom made pick, he pushed it in slowly. Every time he felt the resistance of one of the pins, he levered the pin upwards. Continuing until all the pins were lifted, he kept the pick pushed hard into the lock.

Using the Tension tool, he turned the cylinder until it unlocked. He twisted the cap to make sure it was unlocked. Then he had removed the cap and, reaching under the rubbish on the wheelbarrow, grabbed a gallon plastic container.

The container was two thirds full of oil from his own central heating fuel tank. Quickly fitting the plastic funnel attached to the container, he emptied the heating oil into the fuel tank of Collins' van. Replaced the filler cap and relocked it.

People always assumed it was difficult to pick a lock. It wasn't. All it required was some picks - usually home made although they could be purchased off the internet – and a little bit of finesse.

If people bothered to look on the internet there were even videos showing how to pick locks. Purely as a hobby of course.

Fortunately they didn't or his locksmith company wouldn't have been so successful.

Looking at his watch, he had grinned and congratulated himself. Less than four minutes start to finish. He still had it.

He quickly threw the rubbish into the skip and, making sure the empty fuel container wasn't visible, had returned to his plot. Checking, he had seen that Collins was still deep in conversation with his little informant.

He and Dave both knew that the oil in his central heating tank was almost identical to the fuel in the white van. Almost identical in that both were diesel but with a red dye in the central heating fuel to signify it was for domestic heating or agricultural use.

The significant factor was the price. The diesel oil sold on a fuel forecourt was much dearer because of the government's road fuel tax levy.

By adding a red dye the authorities could quickly determine whether a vehicle was running on legal or illegal diesel oil fuel.

HM Custom and Excise were very interested in people who tried to avoid paying their fuel taxes. Or any tax for that matter.

Consequently they set up exercises where diesel engined vehicles could be checked. Trucks, cars and vans would be diverted into a layby, motorway service area or similar and the contents of their fuel tank checked.

A simple test that involved getting a sample of fuel from the vehicle tank, doing a visual check or adding a chemical and waiting to see if the fuel was Duty Paid or not.

Most offenders were trucks but a significant number of vans and cars were also found to be running on a much cheaper diesel fuel.

Whether the fuel really was cheaper once the significant HM Customs and Excise fine was imposed was debatable.

The other relatively unknown fact about the red dye was that traces of it remained in the vehicle tank long afterwards. So, even if a driver hadn't used "red" diesel for a long time, the chemical the Customs people used still revealed that it *had* been used at some point.

Some unfortunate, yet innocent, people had bought vehicles that had previously been run on red diesel and had still been fined.

Proving that *they* hadn't been the person to put it into the fuel tank was extremely difficult and nearly impossible. It was all down to the attitude of the tax people as to whether you were deemed innocent or guilty.

Now, thanks to him, Collins' van had red diesel in its tank.

Not a problem unless someone phoned up HM Customs and Excise with an anonymous tip off.

Surely no one would do that, he thought with a grin as he reached for his phone. It looked like Operation Get Rid of Collins may be just about to start.

"Hello" he said, " Is that Customs and Excise? I have just seen someone filling up his van's fuel tank from a central heating tank. I was wondering if it is ok to do that? My car is diesel and it would save me having to go to the garage.

It isn't? It's illegal? Oh, I didn't know that. Gosh, that big a fine? Yes, actually I did make a note of the registration number.

My name? Uum, do you really need that? I wouldn't want him finding out it was me that rang you. Yes, I would prefer to remain anonymous. Yes, thank you. No problem. He's not going to be in too much trouble, is he?"

Idly, he wondered how long it would be before Collins had a visit. He decided he would keep his part in this little string operation between Dave and himself. Not that he didn't trust the other guys but why takes chances?

20: The Allotment!

Eamon picked up his van eight days later. I had removed the window film, stickers, red poppy and replaced the original number plates.

Eamon said that he had a customer waiting for the engine. Someone else wanted a back door and then the vehicle would be crushed and sold on as scrap. A couple of days and the duplicate van wouldn't exist.

It didn't matter. It had done its job. I had cruised all the speed camera location I knew about. I had kept my head down so only the peak of my red cap would show on the front shots.

I was pretty sure I had been recorded speeding many times.

A couple of times, when the mobile camera vehicle was set up down my road, I had waited until I saw Collins' van go past.

Then, I followed as quickly as I could and got myself recorded coming and going. Once I even pipped my horn and extended my middle finger as I went past. I did the same in the evenings.

I doubted that Collins kept a log of his allotment trips. He didn't seem to be the type. But, if he decided to challenge the speeding offence times, at least four would be, more or less, in his time frame.

So, there was an impending Customs and Excise visit that would find evidence of red diesel. Then speeding notifications would soon be pouring through his letterbox. I could almost feel sorry for the guy.

Could of ….but didn't. Do unto others as they would do unto you. But do it first, and better.

On the allotment side, there was no progress. My trail camera had recorded nothing of interest other than the allotment did indeed have at least one Muntjac deer.

Plot holders often came across the damage these little deer did. But only a few had actually seen one. I swopped the camera's sd card every few days and uploaded the one that had been recording onto my pc.

The pictures were nice and clear even under infra red conditions. They showed that there was a lot of animal traffic. Dogs, cats, a fox, two Muntjac deer – Labrador dog sized animals with dainty legs and little horns – and a spectacular shot of an owl catching a mouse right in front of the camera.

The was a lot of late evening human traffic. People walking up and down the path. Some recognizably plot holders, other complete strangers.

But despite this, there was no signs of any damage or pilfering being done. I guessed that a lot of the houses adjoining the allotments had access as well. Take advantage of the evening and have a pleasant stroll. Take note of what stuff would soon be ready.

It wasn't until a couple of weeks of recording that Collins began to show up with regularity. Walking up and down with that peculiar rolling walk that easily identified him.

Within easy camera range you could see him stopping at different plots then moving on. Almost like some sort of inspection.

As he moved further away from the camera it was only his walk that suggested it was him. But, other than walking and looking at plots from the path, there was nothing incriminating.

Whenever he walked into camera range, I would freeze frame as he got really close. He seemed to always wear the same clothes and always have the same scowl on his face.

The camera would sometimes catch him walking up the path with Little Mick and there was still no animation on his face. Little Mick was clearly uncomfortable being with him but Collins' expression remained in his seemingly permanent scowl.

I used to tell my kids when they were pulling faces that "if the wind changed, they would stay like that" Perhaps he was scowling when the wind changed?

One of the things about being a truck driver was the opportunities for people watching. Stuck in a traffic jam, waiting to load, unload, embark, disembark, or whatever, you got plenty of time to study people.

You saw people doing all sorts of things when they thought they were unobserved. Drivers tend to forget that, when they are alongside a truck, the trucker can look down into their cars. You see a lot of things as well.

But, mainly you see people reacting to the hold up, traffic jam or whatever has caused the wheels to stop. Pedestrians are interesting to watch as well.

The daily ballet of people avoiding each other. Maintaining the required personal space, the aversion of looking into faces. The late for work, the fed up, the angry, the anxious, the sad, the lonely, the neglected, the keen, the in-loves, the looking for loves and the loves for sale.

After a while of just sitting in a cab and watching people, you begin to recognize and category moods, facial expressions and body language.

What was a way of passing the time becomes a useful tool in daily life. You can define people more easily, recognize a good mood or a bad one.

I felt that I was quite expert at reading people. Which was why I was annoyed with myself for being unable to read Collins more accurately.

Talk to some people down the allotment and they would say he was charming, funny, easy going, helpful and a real nice guy.

Talk to the others – the ones on the end of his temper, viciousness and destructive nature – and another polar image emerged.

Which was the real character of the man? Mr Nice or Mr Nasty? Jekyll or Hyde?

Based on my experience I was going for the Dark Side. The nasty persona was the true Collins, the nice side just a tool to achieve what he wanted. Time to push a little more.

21: The Allotment!

We were all back at the Red Lion in Crick. It was only the second meeting of the Allotmenteers and, hopefully, it would be a more sober affair. And, more productive.

The pub hadn't changed much. Still the same array of old timers and country bumpkins.

Idly, I wondered if the landlord paid them to attend. To give character to the place and boost the Olde Tyme impression and charm. But, looking at our table, people could be forgiven for thinking the same.

Big Mick was the youngest chronologically but blended in seamlessly with us. Fast food and fast drinking had taken an irreversible toll on his youth. Drinks were ordered - individually as agreed - and after a few pleasantries, it was time for our real purpose for being here.

By mutual agreement, Pete and I kept our little bits of mischief quiet. I knew about Pete's, having planned it with him, but he was ignorant of mine.

Both were criminal acts and not something to be broadcast. I didn't trust the other guys enough yet.

Of course, the first thing that came up was our Dress up like Collins exercise. We had all continued to wear braces and baseball caps when working on our plots. Big Mick, well into his third pint, still thought it hilarious. I asked for ideas of a similar nature. Or bigger.

Paul started first. " Have you noticed that Bert paints his sheds red?" he asked. It was hard not to miss that Fire Engine red. It stood out like a burning beacon. We all nodded.

"Well, he painted his big shed that colour when it was on the Dunchurch allotment. The Allotment Committee asked everyone to paint their sheds green, sort of like a uniform, but Bert painted his red in defiance. The Committee didn't like it and that was the final straw.

When he came to our allotments, about five years ago, he rebuilt the shed. It was still painted red, of course.

Then, when he got his second plot he bought another shed for that one. Second hand out of the local paper. He painted that red as well but, because it was new paint, it made his original shed look a bit dull." Paul sipped at his pint. Took off his cap and wiped his head with a tissue.

"Anyway he ended up painting the other shed as well. But, strangely, he moved it to the other side of the plot first. None of us could the reasoning behind it. Why would you move a shed after two years? It was in its original place one night and when Old Fred, I think it was, – you remember Old Fred and his huge tomatoes don't' you? – came in at seven the next morning Collins had nearly finished moving it. Why do you think that was?" Paul looked around the table.

"Because the guy's an idiot." Big Mick replied.

"Well, we know he's not an idiot. And to be fair, he has two great plots. He didn't just move it on a whim" Adrian mused. " There's always a reason with Collins. The only reason I can think of is that it made his shed more visible from the main gate. Sort of a giant red exclamation mark."

"What, you mean like an "up yours" sort of thing?" Paul asked. " I had that same thought as well. But, the main reason I mentioned it is because it must have been done for a reason. I just can't thing of one but it was important enough to him to do it."

"Yeah, well?" Big Mick asked with the careful speech of someone who has had a few.

"Well, what if we all got together one night and painted both sheds a different colour? Let him come down one morning and see his sheds painted....?"

"Black" "Camel Breath Green" "In underseal or tar" were the suggestions from around the table. Camel Breath Green was mine. I had once seen a car advert describing the car's colour and it had stuck.

"What about Candy Pink?" Paul said with a big grin on his face. "Two sheds in a very bright Candy Pink. Can you imagine his expression?"

Obviously everyone could because there was laughter and back slapping all round. Even the old timers looked up from their seemingly everlasting matchstick game.

" I guess because you were so specific about what colour pink that you just happen to have some?" I asked Paul when the merriment had died down.

He had. Two whole tins in his garage. Left over from when he was asked to paint his grand daughter's bedroom. Her mum had ordered it off Ebay and had instantly changed her mind once the lid had been prised open and her eyeballs were singed.

A quick trip to Do It All and a more muted shade of pink was now on her walls. It would have cost more to send the tins back than they were worth. So they had been in his garage ever since.

Like most of us old guys, Paul hated throwing anything out on the basis "that it might come in handy, one day." Lynne is always getting on to me about keeping stuff. I always tell her the same thing as well.

Well, for once, Paul had been proved right.

There was no more discussions or ideas thrown about after that. Almost by design, we each looked at each other and nodded. Right. No time like the present. Still light outside.

Half an hour after we had arrived, we were pulling out of the Red Lion's car park. Ten minutes later, we pulled into the Victory allotments car park.

Minus Paul who had gone home to fetch paint, paintbrushes, rollers and paint trays.

He quickly returned and unloaded. We transferred everything to the two plots and started. The first thing we did after opening the tins was stare in shocked awe.

Have you seen that scene in the Indiana Jones film, Raiders of the lost Ark, when the Ark of the Covenant is opened? There is a blindingly bright light coming from the lid and a heavenly chorus.

Well it was a bit like that. Except there was no heavenly chorus. There was a lot of more down to earth comments of the profane variety.

Candy Pink, we discovered, was indeed bright. The sort of pink that should have come with a Health Warning: "Caution, may damage your eyeballs" type of thing.

Hard to describe the exact shade except to say it was luminous, horrendously pink and should have come with dark glasses as standard.

Peel your eyeballs Pink or Profanity Pink might have been more apt. Particularly the latter judging by the less than complimentary remarks.

It was just perfect.

Surprisingly, despite all the giggles and side splitting laughter, the whole job only took just under an hour of sploshing, flinging and rollering paint.

It wouldn't have won any Best Painting awards. There were numerous runs – like the Cresta bob sleigh run for example – and paint dripping off the roof in long, unhealthy looking glutinous strings.

Maybe it would have been a better job if we hadn't been to the pub first. Or if Big Mick hadn't brought along a trio of now empty lager six packs.

I found out, when you were thirsty and decorating, that the taste of lager became quite acceptable after a couple or four cans. It tends to make you feel a bit wobbly though.

Nor had any of us escaped unscathed. Adrian had pink highlights in his white hair.

The peak of Paul's flat cap was tastefully edged in pink where it had fallen into a can.

Pete's face was peppered with pink spots.

Big Mick had a pink backside where he had tripped and fallen seat first into a tray of paint.

My clothes were a clear demonstration of why it was best to buy cheap from charity shops and just discard once they had been pressed against a wet, pink painted, shed.

None of us minded. There were hugs, big grins, laughter and back slaps as we stood at the gate and surveyed our handiwork.

The two sheds stood smoldering in their new finery. Pink and Proud. As a final touch, Adrian had hurried home and returned with a spray can of black paint.

As neatly as he could – or anyone who had consumer too much larger and couldn't really see because of the tears of laughter in his eyes was able – he had named the bigger shed "The Peedo Pad" and the smaller one boasted the legend "The Homo's Home".

I guess spelling wasn't Adrian's - he of the pink and white hair -   best subject at school.

Tomorrow, everyone agreed, would be interesting. We said our goodbyes. I reminded everyone to get rid of all traces of pink.

I gave Big Mick an old towel I kept in Lynne's car to protect his seat.

I stripped off my outer wear and donned some overalls I keep in her boot for emergencies. The clothes went into a plastic bag and then down the chute and into the rubbish container in the car park.

I got into the car and cast one last look at our handiwork. Couldn't help smiling. I might get down here a little earlier tomorrow, I thought.

Back at the house, I was greeted with "Surely you haven't gone out dressed like that?" And, after much sniffing. "Have you been drinking?"

"No, of course not." I replied as I put the kettle on. "A couple of shandies. And, as for my overalls, you know I like to dress up when I go out. I was just down my shed looking for something and didn't want to get my best clobber dirty. "

Lynne looked at me. "That explains why you don't go out much. And, why are your hands pink? What is that colour? It's horrible."

"Oh, I was just down the workshop and I found this tin of paint. I thought I would use it to freshen up the spare bedroom."

"You do that and you'll be sleeping in it." She warned as she picked up my cup of tea and returned to her computer and Farmville, Facethingy, Twatter or whatever it was she found so fascinating.

I made myself another cup of tea.

22: The Allotment!

Albert Collins was just about to go to the allotment when the glass panel in the front door darkened. He could see someone wearing dark clothes and some sort of hat. There was more movement behind the dark shape. A sharp rat tat tat on the glass panel seemed to echo through the house.

He opened the door and saw a policeman standing full square in front of him. Behind him there were two more people. An older man in a dark blue uniform and a young lady, more a girl, in jeans and sweater.

"Mr Collins? Mr Albert Collins?" the young policeman asked.

"Yeah, whadda you want?"

"Are you the owner of a white Vauxhall van, registration number BV03 WHT?" the officer was looking pointedly at the white van parked on the drive.

"Yeah. What about it? It's taxed until the end of next month, mot'd and insured. I can show you the documents."

The officer looked at the notebook in his hand "Yes, I know. We are not here about that. We have had a phone call saying that you are running it on red diesel."

"That's bloody rubbish. I always fill up at Sainsbury's. So, unless supermarkets are selling red diesel, you're wasting your time." Collins was getting angry. After the last time, he didn't like the police coming round to his house. And most certainly not for something as trivial as the colour of the diesel his van ran on. "Who rang you? Was it one of my neighbours?"

"I'm afraid that is confidential, Sir. So you are saying that the allegation is untrue?"

"Course it's untrue. Do I look stupid? Now, if you don't mind, I have to go"

"Unfortunately, the allegation has been made. If it is untrue then you have nothing to worry about, have you, Sir? So you wouldn't mind if these officers from HM Customs and Excise took a quick sample, would you? It won't take long and it would clear the matter up."

"Take your sample and hurry up. Don't you people have anything better to do that harass people?"

"Thank you Sir." The young lady said as she opened a large case on the floor beside her. "This won't take long. Do you have the key to the fuel cap? Otherwise we will have to force it."

Collins fished in his pocket, removed his keys, selected one and handed it over.

He watched as the girl's companion removed the filler cap.

The girl inserted a plastic syphon tube , pumped the flattened top and a steam of diesel came from the secondary tube at the top into a glass container her companion held.

When the container was two thirds full, she stopped pumping and, with a practised move, removed the syphon without spilling any diesel.

Returning to her case, she extracted a small phial of colourless liquid which she poured into the glass container. She gave the container a swirl to mix the two liquids and then inspected the result. As Collins watched, the clear diesel changed to a slightly cloudy red colour.

Nodding to her companions, she turned to Collins. "Positive for red diesel, Sir. Perhaps you would like to explain just why you are running your vehicle on untaxed red diesel?"

With bulging eyes Collins looked at the container and then back to the girl. "You've done the test wrong, you stupid girl. I haven't been running on red diesel."

Unperturbed, the girl turned to her companion. "Would you like to write it out?" she asked.

"Write what out? What the hell are you talking about?"

"You are charged with running your vehicle on fuel which hasn't been taxed for road use. In other words, you are avoiding Excise Duty and that is a serious offence under Section 9 of the Finance Act 1994." The police officer told him. " I must caution you that anything you say may be taken down and used in evidence against you........."

Stunned, Collins stood whilst he was cautioned. He looked from one to the other hoping it was a mistake.

"What…. What happens now?" he stuttered. "You can't do this….this is a mistake……I'm going to get a solicitor onto you.. you won't get away with it…."

"That is probably a good thing, Sir" the police man told him. "It's a serious offence and the courts have the authority to impose a maximum 7 year prison sentence, an unlimited fine or both. Your vehicle is also liable for seizure. Thank you for your co-operation, sir. We will be in touch in due course. Good day."

The older man finished writing and held a clipboard under his nose "Would you like to sign this, Sir?" he asked the bewildered Collins. " Just there at the bottom. I'll give you a copy for your records. Thank you , Sir. Good day." He ripped off a printed form and handed it over.

In a daze, Collins watched as the trio walked down his path. Just as they exited onto the street, the postman walked up to him. "What you been up to then?" he asked jovially handing over some letters.

"Mind your own business." Collins snarled as he snatched the four envelopes from him. Still in a daze, he looked at them.

One was promising him unlimited broadband. Another reminded him that his road tax was due next month.

The other two each contained a summons for speeding.

*****

I was just putting my coat on when the phone rang. I was going down the allotment to witness the results of last night's labours.

For some reason I had a headache and my mouth felt like one of the dogs had been moulting in it. Must have been the paint.

I didn't pick up because the staff usually answers. Phone calls in our house are hardly ever for me anyway.

"Aren't you going to get that?" the dulcet tones of the blight of my life asked. Or should that have been Light of my life.

"Me? Get to answer a phone call? Are you feeling ok?" You just can't get the staff these days. I haven't picked up a phone in months. The staff usually find me and hand it over. I remembered how to answer and heard the echoey noise of a mobile.

"Dave?.....it's Anne. Anne Wood. ..Yes, we're fine. How are you both? Ah, good. Listen I won't hold you up."

The connection was a bit patchy but I could hear Liverpudlian Charlie Landsborough singing "What colour is the wind?" softly in the background.

I think Anne was secretly in love with Charlie. A bit like Lynne with Quiff Richard. Anne's voice faded in and out.

"Hallo? Are you there? I keep losing the signal….. Oh, that's better. Look, I know we were meant to be coming up next week but we are on our way now." Her voice was crackly and faded in and out.

 "Joe had to come up to Coventry anyway so we are going combine things. Will you be able to arrange things at such short notice? It doesn't matter if you can't…… are you sure? Ok, thanks. We'll see you in about half an hour."

Joe and Anne Trent were friends of cousin, Carolyn. They live in Tonbridge down in Kent. One of the posher areas of the county.

We met initially at the house of one of my cousins when they, and we, were both visiting.

I got talking to Joe and discovered that he had a love and a passion for classic and vintage cars. At that time he had a classic 1954 Bristol 403 in a dark red which he had just got. His other car was a vintage 1933 Austin Twelve Harley in a two tone blue and black.

I asked him about the difference between a vintage and a classic car.

Basically a vintage car is manufactured between 1919-1930 in the UK but up to 1935 in the USA and other countries. A classic, in the UK definition, is a post war vehicle no longer in production.

He told me that there is a lot of disputes between the definitions because a year either side can mean more or less value for your car.

Since we both had an interest in vehicles, we hit it off. He was in Local Government and had retired as a Chief Accountant. Really though, he had always wanted to be a mechanic.

He restored and tinkered with cars as a hobby and even became a race scrutineer for the RAC in the Formula classification of racing.

He raced vintage cars himself in his 50's but a nasty crash convinced him it was time stop. Even now in his 70's he still tours and attends car rallies with his wife of 37 years.

Because of my motoring journalist connections I had a lot of contacts. A couple of weeks back, Anne had rung me to ask about the Coventry Museum of Transport.

She had heard about it and wanted to surprise Joe on his birthday. Her idea was a posh hotel and a visit to the museum. I knew quite a lot about the place because the guy who was in charge was a press friend/contact of mine.

Basically the Museum has a collection of British made road transport vehicles comprising of around 240 cars and commercial vehicles, 100 motor cycles and a huge collection of bicycles.

She asked me about admission prices and was astonished to find out the entry was free and included guided tours.

What she didn't know was that I had contacted my mate and arranged for the two old codgers to have an unrestricted, all areas, V.I.P type tour of the facility.

This meant that they would be allowed to see the old vehicles being repaired and restored in the workshops prior to being on view. Something not normally on the tour.

Given Joe's passion for restoring, I felt that this would be something he would appreciate.

Now, I had to ring and ask if it was still possible even at such short notice. It was. Another favour owed.

Barely twenty minutes later, they were at the front door. Joe looks a bit like Captain Birdseye with his white hair and beard, glasses and peaked motoring cap.

Anne was everyone's fantasy of the perfect grandmother. White hair and smiley face with a laugh always bubbling just below the surface. The sort of lady you instinctively wanted to hug. The Aunt Bessie of Tonbridge.

She was smaller than Joe, with similar white hair – no beard - and very active with inquisitive eyes and an engaging personality. Even if you had just met her, you felt you had always known her and wanted her to be your friend.

She was in her mid 70's and had been, like Joe, in Local Government as a secretary. She had to leave mid-career to look after first, her parents, and then Joe's father. All alongside caring for her own children, her grandchildren and the myriad friends she attracted.

Now she and Joe liked to travel in their cars, attend rallies, spoil the grandchildren and, generally, grow old disgracefully.

I like to think I am active for my age but would be hard pushed to keep up with them.

This pair of old whiteheads had just driven up from Kent in an even older car and were still full of energy. Even to the point of asking if they could have a look at my allotment.

Even as Joe asked me, a thought popped into my head. A "me and my warped sense of humour" thought. They had a cup of tea and we left.

Lynne stayed as she had a dental appointment in half an hour. I did offer to drop her teeth off for her. For some reason she was not amused.

I said it would be better if Joe and Anne took the car. My back had been playing up a bit – no doubt after last night's shenanigans – so I told them I would walk to get the kinks out. I had a bit of a headache as well for some reason.

I gave them directions and said I would meet them in the car park. That way they could go straight onto Coventry without having to walk back to our house.

On the walk down, I was eagerly anticipating Collins' reaction to our remodeling of his sheds.

An old blue and black Austin passed me with a throaty pip from its horn. Anne gave a regal wave as they passed.

Old cars tend to make people look like royalty for some reason. I like looking at old cars but prefer my vehicular comfort these days.

I walked through the back gates and down the path. At the far end I could see the Allotmenteers milling around trying not to look conspicuous.

In fact, looking around, I could see that there were a lot of High End people just pretending to be busy or standing in groups. I had never seen the allotments this full before.

Big Mick anticipated my question. "I might have told a few people in the pub last night." Again he anticipated me. "I popped in for a quick one after I had changed my clothes. Word must have spread. And, no, I didn't say anything else. I just said someone had told me."

Before I could say anything else, I was being asked questions of the. "Any sign of him?" "He's not normally this late. Do you think something has happened?" variety.

I told them I was going to the main gate to let my friends in. I mentioned that they had a vintage Austin and they enthusiastically trooped down with me.

The first thing that caught my eye were the two Pink Palaces. You couldn't ignore them. I reckon if you Googled the allotments on Earth Search they would show up.

They had already attracted a lot of interest. A lot, if not most, of the Lower End plot people were pretending to work on their plots but were more interested in looking at our handiwork.

In the full light of day, they looked horrendous. Pink and very, very Proud. It was also obvious that the Allotmenteers weren't very good at painting and decorating.

Runs on the roof looked like ridges. There were thick pinkicles hanging down like old, forgotten Christmas decorations. There were lots of places where the paint had missed completely. But, overall, the work had achieved its purpose. You just could not miss them.

Even a blind man would be able to feel the Pinkness radiating and overwhelming him. If his dog could be persuaded to go any where near them that is.

I had a vision of a Labrador dog running full pelt up the path dragging its owner behind. My weird sense of humour found that funny.

But, if nothing else, we had cheered everyone up. There was more laughter, smiles and chuckles down this area in one morning than in the history of the allotments. I suddenly remembered my guests.

Anne and Joe were as gobsmacked as every one else. Anne had her camera out and was busy taking pictures. "Is the owner colour blind?" she asked.

"It wasn't like that yesterday." I told her. "Probably some vandal's idea of fun. I don't think the owner will be best pleased when he gets here."

I introduced my gang to them. We ended up in a group around the venerable Austin. We admired the immaculate bodywork, the running boards, the wire spoked wheels and bulging headlights.

We opened the doors to look inside. The first thing that hit us was that wonderful smell that old cars have and that modern vehicles with their synthetic interiors don't.

The smell of old leather, kids being sick, the fumblings, the frantic couplings, the heat, the cold, the memories of distant journeys that all the old natural materials soak up, retain and then release down Memory Lane when the doors are opened.

Everyone agreed that "they don't make them like that anymore."

Pete remembered that his dad had one just like it. "We used to go everywhere in it. Days out at the seaside. Runs in the country. People used to drive for pleasure in those days. They wouldn't now."

Because we were all of a certain age, we all had memories of the golden days of motoring when petrol was cheap and the roads not congested.

"Everything was cheap in those days?" Adrian reminisced. "You could go out for the night with a few pennies in your pocket and have a good time." Everyone's head was nodding in mutual agreement.

" Go to the pictures, buy your bird a few drinks in the pub afterwards, get fish and chips on the way home and still have money left." Paul chipped in.

"You could go into a supermarket, get the groceries and still have money in your pocket." Pete said. "You can't do that these days. CCTV has a lot to answer for, doesn't it?" he mused. That got a few laughs.

"Yes, things are tight all round these days" Joe joined in. " I was reading just the other day that Rabbis in the synagogues don't get paid for performing circumcisions any more." He looked around. "Apparently they have to be content with the tips."

He had said it so seriously that it took a minute for what he had said to sink in. First one and then another got it until everyone was laughing. Apart from Anne. She had probably heard it before.

We were still laughing when a white van turned up and parked next to the Austin. Collins got out and glowered at us. " I usually park there." He growled.

"Well, you don't today." I replied. "Not our fault you are late. Besides, I didn't know there was reserved parking here. I thought it was on a first come, nearer the gate, basis."

Collins was trying to avoid looking at me as he removed a fork from the back of his van. Without another word, he shouldered past us and walked towards the gate.

It was as if he had walked into a brick wall. He just stopped dead as he saw his sheds. His shoulders sagged and the fork dropped to the ground.

He turned to us, turned back and turned again. His mouth was working but there was no sound coming out. His face flushed and his shaggy eyebrows seemed knitted together.

He pulled the gate open and rushed up to his big shed. Slowly, unbelievingly, he prodded it with a shaking finger. Held the finger up to his eyes as if giving us the finger. He slowly turned, as if in a daze, as someone lower down the path tried to stifle a laugh and failed. It came out as more of a dry croak.

That seemed to be the trigger. Suddenly, everyone was laughing and pointing. Collins looked this way and that as he tried desperately to take it all in. He saw nothing but laughing faces or pink wherever he looked.

First of all the diesel, then the speeding fines and now….. this.

Suddenly his temper boiled out and he found his voice.

"Ooh, you bastards. " he shouted as he looked at each face trying to find a clue as to who was responsible. "You'll all pay for this. I'll make you all sorry. Think this is funny, do you?" he snarled at the nearest laughing face. "Try this for funny." He said as he came closer and punched the unlucky man in the face.

The laughter all stopped as the guy dropped like a stone. Still Collins wasn't finished. He lashed out with his heavy boots at the unmoving body on the floor. Again and again he kicked.

Suddenly he was surrounded by angry people as, with one accord, they closed up around him. Several people grabbed him and held his arms in strong grips as they dragged him away from his victim.

Some went to the fallen man's aid. Others began to punch Collins as they unleashed their anger at both the senseless attack and the hostility they harboured against him.

Suddenly it seemed as if Collins was lost in a sea of punches, kicks and angry shouting men.

I looked at my group. Without a word being spoken we went to the aid of the man we all hated. We pulled people away from him and then surrounded him. Protected him

We shouted for everyone to stop and for someone to call an ambulance for the unconscious man still lying on the ground. Gradually the mob rage dissipated and people began to return to normal.

An ambulance was called and someone pulled Dereck – as I found he was called – into the recovery position and covered him with a coat.

In the meantime, we pulled Collins to his van, shoved him in and told him to go while he had the chance.

His nose was bleeding, one eye was closing and he had several abrasions on his face.

He left without another word, kangaroo hopping out of the car park as his shaking legs tried to control the pedals. We were silent and subdued as we watched him go.

I belatedly remembered Joe and Anne. They were stood by their car. Joe had his arms around Anne and was stroking her hair as he tried to sooth her.

I quickly made sure they were all right and hadn't been injured in any way. They were both shocked but unhurt. I tried to explain to them what had just happened.

How a bunch of men had finally turned against a guy who had constantly bullied and belittled them. I didn't mention our part in the catalyst.

The sound of sirens came down the road and soon the ambulance was turning into the car park.

Someone had thought to stand by the road to guide it in. The crew were quickly told what had happened and were soon treating the now conscious Dereck.

Fortunately there didn't appear to be anything broken but they decided to take him to the hospital for x rays just in case. Every one was subdued as the ambulance left.

By now Anne had recovered and back to her amiable self. She held up her camera. "I was taking pictures of the sheds." She said. "It all happened so quickly. I've just been looking and I have taken quite a lot of photos. I must have kept my finger pressed down on the button."

She scrolled though the pictures and had indeed taken a lot. There were several of Collins kicking Dereck and one lucky shot of his fist hitting the unfortunate guy's face.

"Look, I'm sorry about this." I said. "It's not normally like this. I hope it hasn't stopped you going to Coventry?" I looked at them anxiously.

"No, these things happen." Joe said. "We're just glad nobody was really hurt. One thing…" he said with a lopsided grin "….we won't forget this trip in a hurry and we haven't even got to Coventry yet."

They agreed that they would go as planned. I whispered to Anne to ask for my friend at the museum and give my name.

"Thanks for this" she said as we hugged goodbye. "I'll send you some pictures when we get back. Do you want me to send you the ones I've just taken as well?" she asked with a nod at the pink sheds.

I thought that might be a good idea and she said she would email them when she got home. I shook Joe's hand and watched as they drove off.

I turned to the silent and shaken Allotmenteers. "How do you think that went? " I asked.

I think we were all surprised by how quickly it had kicked off. How quickly normally placid men had turned into a lynch mob.

I'm not even sure just what we had expected. Last night it had seemed like a good idea. Right now, we felt relieved that no one had been more seriously hurt.

Collins had acted as we had anticipated. Just more quickly and viciously than we had thought. I imagine we expected a temper tantrum, shouting and threatening but nothing like this.

I remembered the thought I had before coming down here. The idea that my warped sense of humour thought might be funny.

To have Anne and Joe pretend to be from a gardening magazine and to wander around judging the plots for a "Best Allotment" competition.

To stand at Collins' allotments, look at the pink sheds and pointedly shake their heads as he watched. Then have them go to one of the scruffy adjacent plots and loudly enthuse about its "natural untouched beauty" and such like.

I felt relieved that it hadn't happened. Collins could just as quickly have lashed out at them.

As I said, I have a warped sense of humour that Lynne says will get me into trouble one day.

Thankfully, it wasn't today but it was close. Too close.

23: The Allotment!

Getting out of bed the next morning was a major problem for Albert Collins. He hurt all over and could barely straighten up.

In the bathroom's grimy mirror he saw two swollen purple eyes, bulbous nose, blue and yellow facial bruises and various cuts and scrapes.

His torso also had numerous and similar technicolour marks where angry boots and fists had landed.

The pain from his ribs was sharp and intense when he breathed. He had to breathe through his mouth because his nose was so swollen. But, he knew that the aches and pains would lessen and go in time.

But, he wondered, how long the fear and confusion he felt would take to go away. If ever.

He was so used to having people scared of him that he had forgotten what it felt like to be afraid. He usually inflicted pain on others not the other way round.

He could still remember the surprise he had felt when the normally placid and frightened plot holders had pulled him away from the guy who had laughed in his face.

Not only pulled him away but had held him as they punched, pummeled and kicked him.

That was when the surprise had changed to fear. Him, afraid of those morons.

Even worse was the humiliation of knowing that the group he held responsible for the change of attitude down the allotments had rescued him.

Pulled him away, put him in his van and told him to go. And he had. Couldn't get away quickly enough if the truth be known.

He remembered that he couldn't control the pedals properly because his legs were shaking so much.

How he had lurched out of the car park and up the road.

How he had to stop and be sick onto the road.

The copious amounts of vomit and then the dry heaving as the fear induced adrenalin left his body.

He hadn't slept much last night. It wasn't just because of the pain, the humiliation and the fear.

In the early hours he had suddenly realised that he couldn't go back to the allotments.

He couldn't face the sight of his defaced sheds, the knowing looks and laughter of those around him. Whether they were laughing at him or not.

And, if he couldn't go back there then he couldn't stay here. It was too risky. He had to get away. But where? Just where could he go?

He slowly and painfully descended the stairs and into the kitchen. Made himself a cup of tea and some toast. Sat at his dilapidated table and looked around his dirty kitchen as he ate and drank.

He realised that there was really nothing of value in the house. It was all his parents furniture and had probably been second hand when they got it.

The house belonged to the council and, apart from his van and some tools, he had nothing of real value in his life.

There really was nothing to stop him loading up his van and leaving.

Where would he go? Did it matter? He could just go wherever the fancy took him.

He had a fairly healthy bank account that would keep him for some time. He could kip in his van, in cheap b&b's or an off-season caravan park.

There was a tow bar on his van so why not just get a caravan? In fact he could trade in his van for something bigger. Another van or even consider a campervan. He could live quite comfortably in one of those.

Maybe go down south or even the continent? Go to Spain and live on the beach. He knew some people down near Malaga. Maybe stop with them until he got sorted? The cost of living was cheaper and there would be plenty of opportunities in Spain.

Suddenly things looked brighter. He had more or less decided he was going to leave. Just needed a little push to make up his mind.

He heard the mail flap click and then the sound of letters hitting the hallway floor.

Rising carefully from the chair, he hobbled down the grimy hallway and picked up five brown envelopes.

He stared at them and suddenly had an insight of what they contained.

Back in the kitchen, he furiously ripped them open and laid them out on the table. He looked at the identical envelope and its content still there from yesterday.

Counted five, no six, speeding tickets. Just what the hell was going on? Suddenly, just like that, he made up his mind.

To Hell with them. To Hell with everything. He was out of here.

But, first, he some things to do. Sort out those bloody coppers and their poxy speeding tickets.

Then settle a few scores down on the allotment.

24: The Allotment!

Everyone was very subdued down the allotments the next morning. My gang were grouped on Adrian's plot. They were having a brew made on the gas ring in his shed.

The council didn't encourage gas containers as they were considered a fire hazard. Most of the plot holders had some sort of fire hazard on their plots whether gas containers, petrol containers for lawnmowers, strimmers and cultivators or just plain fertilizer.

But, obviously today's topic was not about fire hazards but about what had happened yesterday. There was no doubt that painting Collins' sheds had triggered it.

There was equally no doubt that we had saved Collins from a more severe beating or worse.

I have seen mob frenzy at football matches and what happened yesterday was very similar. Men with their blood up and looking to vent their anger on something or someone.

Dereck was apparently, apart from bruising and sore ribs, none the worse for his ordeal. X-rays revealed that nothing was broken. He was discharged and told to take it easy for a few days. According to Big Mick, his missus had been in touch with the police and the council.

Which led to our next big decision. Whether we owned up to being the catalyst or not.

After a lot of discussion it was decided that nothing good would come from owning up. People might suspect who had painted the sheds but were unlikely to be able to prove it. And, why would they?

Yesterday's violence was something everyone would want to forget. If we stood up for one crime it was likely that someone's conscience would make him own up to his part. And, once one person started relieving his conscience, others would be drawn in as well.

So, in the end it was decided that more good would come from saying nothing than owning up. And, it wasn't from fear of the consequences.

Our crime was hardly jail time material. Maybe a slap on the wrist, a fine and probably getting chucked off the allotment.

And the only one that would benefit would be Collins who could claim provocation for his temper outburst and subsequent violence.

If we all stuck together - and that meant everyone involved in the incident – and said nothing then our ultimate aim of getting rid of Collins looked very likely.

It was felt that Collins, knowing now how everyone felt about him, was unlikely to return.

The humiliation of everyone knowing that he had been beaten and thrown off the allotment would be just too great.

So, everyone decided to say nothing and await developments.

*****

John Burns didn't know what to do. The wife of one of the Victory Allotment plot holders had been in touch first thing.

A very angry Mrs. Derecek Blainey had demanded to know just what the council was going to do about that monster who viciously attacked her husband yesterday and put him in hospital.

She further informed him that she had been to the police to start criminal charges and was seeing a solicitor to see who to sue for her husband's injuries.

Injuries, she informed him furiously, that took place on council property and by a council tenant.

Actually he did know what to do. He had no choice in the matter. He had to act quickly and decisively.

He looked up the contact number and rang. "Hello. Is that Dave? Can you tell me just what happened down the allotments yesterday? I've had the wife of a tenant on the phone this morning threatening to sue because her husband was beaten up yesterday. Do you know anything about it? Where you there? Who was responsible?"

Great. I'd barely got home as well. Good job I'd had the chance to meet the other guys first. At least we would all be singing from the same hymn sheet.

As concisely as possible I told Burns what I knew. That someone had painted Collins' sheds the previous afternoon or evening. That he had seen his sheds and gone berserk. Grabbing the unlucky Dereck and proceeding to punch and kick him.

How the other tenants had pulled him off and began to administer their own punching and kicking.

How my group of Top End neighbours had rescued Collins and advised him to leave.

"So, most of the tenants either witnessed it or joined in?" He asked after a long pause once I had finished with the bare facts. "And Collins definitely kicked off first? And no one has any idea of who defaced his sheds?

Well, it seems I haven't a lot of choice. I'll have to tell Collins he has to go. No other choice, is there?/"

"Well, it doesn't seem so." I cautiously agreed with him. " He definitely started it and it could have got nasty. But, the thing is, how is this going to affect you personally?"

Burns seemed a different person to the one I'd spoken to previously. More assured, decisive, more....well, in command of himself.

"I'd already made my decision in that respect. I've told my wife, told her my affair is over, and we are trying to work something out together.

But, I'd already decided that I would leave and try to start elsewhere if things didn't work out here.

You were right, better to face things than live in fear of them." He told me.

"I might need a statement or something from you and some of the other witnesses. Right, better go and face my boss. He'll want to try to keep this quiet if possible.

I'd appreciate it if you and the others didn't say anything damaging to the press.

We'll try and keep a lid on it. That way we might not have to try and find out who painted those damn sheds." Did I detect a warning in his tone? He carried on... "The colour? Is the colour really that bad?"

I might have imagined it but I could have sworn I heard the start of a laugh before the line went dead.

*****

Collins had gone storming, or as quickly as his stiffness allowed, into Rugby police station.

At the counter he had demanded to know who had issued the speeding tickets and what proof they had.

He had left some twenty minutes later totally confused. He had shut up pretty quickly when he saw the speed camera photos.

There was no doubt it was his van and no doubt that the driver, what little could be seen of the face beneath the baseball cap, could be him. But how? He hadn't been where many of the offences were said to have taken place in weeks. Yet there were the photos. Date and time stamped with location and the over the limit speed at the time of the offence.

And, the copper in charge of that department had curtly told him, there were a few more in the system he would be receiving in the near future.

Together with the red diesel charge, he would be looking at a huge amount of fines and almost certainly lose his licence.

Depending on the magistrate, a custodial sentence might well be on the cards as well, the Jobsworth had cheerfully informed him. The courts were already clamping down hard on speeding motorists. Particularly, the more persistent ones.

He was thinking hard about his future when he got back to his van.

He wasn't best pleased to find a parking ticket on his windscreen. It was that little piece of paper in it's sticky plastic envelope that finally decided him.

25: The Allotment!.

It hadn't been a bad winter. More freezing temperatures than blanketing snow. Along with everyone else down the allotments, I had spent the last weeks of Autumn preparing for the winter months.

I hoed, weeded, tidied up and dug over any bare patches. Dig before the winter, I was told by some smarmy guy on the tv, and the frost and snow will break up the soil for you. Then it will only need a little raking in the Spring to get your beds ready for planting, he said.

Anything left growing was either picked, frozen, dumped in the compost or skipped.

The brussel sprouts and cabbages were left as the tv smarmy bloke said they improved with a few sharp frosts.

On the plus side it was a nice "All my own work. Grown with my own hands" smug feeling when everyone said nice things about the sprouts we had with our Christmas dinner.

I used to come down a couple of times a week just for a walk and to check everything was ok.

I had started taking one of our Yorkshire Terrier dogs, Zak, with me and now couldn't reach for my wellies without him fetching his lead.

As soon as I entered the back gate, I would let him off his lead. Once he startled a Muntjac deer and chased it. He changed his mind when the deer turned round and put his head down. They have some sharp looking little curved horns.

But, generally, Zak and I were the only ones down there. As I walked down the path towards my patch, I looked at the other plots.

Little Mick had left. Just upped forks and left and his patch was now empty. John Burns was still in charge and he told me that there were a lot of new tenants waiting to be given vacant plots and the keys to the gates.

John and I got on well now. He became a more "hands on" type of manager and usually tried to sort out any problems quickly and efficiently. I was glad he had worked his personal life problems out.

Many of the other plots were shut up for the winter. The tenants would no doubt re-appear in the Spring blinking and pale from their long winter hibernation.

I stopped briefly at my patch to check things were ok. I planned to get a shed sorted for the spring. Nothing as big as the last one. Something like an 8' x6' size. Big enough to store tools and things.

I had already acquired a gas ring, kettle and drink making stuff. It was kept in my Command Centre in readiness for the Big Day.

My elder daughter was throwing out some plastic chairs so they were ready to move in as well.

The staff has started to express an interest in taking a more active interest in OUR allotment. Probably more in the supervisory area than the hands on, down and dirty, end.

She has already got the pink – unfortunate colour choice – patterned wellies and the designer gardening gloves recommended by Mr Smarmy on the gardening programme.

She has also been looking at some nice shiny chrome plated spades and forks. Oh, and an intense interest in gardening catalogues, packets of seeds and planting schedules.

Zak raced down the path to the main gate then raced back. He was only small but he could shift. I could just see the remains of Big Mick and Paul's sheds after the fires.

They were going to be replaced in the spring as well. The fires had started two nights after the Pink Shed incident. Everyone guessed who had started them but, this time, they didn't have to speculate.

My little, almost forgotten, hidden trail camera had carried on filming and recording onto its memory card. I had taken it home and played the sd card in my pc.

Besides the usual assortments of allotment people, walkers and night animals there was a couple of nice shots of a not so nice night animal.

Albert Collins walking down the path with a fuel can in one hand and a plastic bag in the other.

Then, according to the time index, ten minutes later returning with fuel can and no plastic bag.

On the return journey he was very nicely framed by the increasingly fierce flames from a couple of sheds.

I ran two lots of prints off and gave one set to John Burns. He passed them onto the police.

When they eventually turned up at Collins' house in Dunchurch, they found it empty. They knocked on his neighbours door and was told that he had turned up with a new camper type van, loaded some plastic bags and suitcases and driven off. They hadn't seen him since.

The police returned a month later to serve a summons for unpaid speeding tickets and one parking fine.

He wasn't there either when they turned up three of months later with a more serious purpose.

The new tenants had only moved in a week previously after the council had repossessed its property, thoroughly cleaned, decorated and then re-let it.

It was purely co-incidental that the police called that last time. But no coincidence that the matter didn't stop there. Nor that a lot of time and manpower was involved in trying to find the elusive Mr Collins.

*****

Anne Trent had sent me the Pink Sheds and punch up photos in an email when she returned from their very satisfying trip to the Coventry Motor Museum.

Joe had been suitably thrilled with his behind the scenes tour and comparing his Austin to a similar exhibit model. He reckoned that his car just had the edge.

In the e-mail she thanked me and then told me of a funny co-incidence when showing her Polish neighbour the Pink Sheds shots.

The neighbour had a friend from nearby Seven Oaks visiting and she said something to her in Polish. Probably along the lines of "Come and see what colour the crazy English paint their sheds."

The visiting friend had laughed and commented suitably about the colour choice and then seemed to freeze and look more closely.

Then she had gone to the next room and returned with her handbag. Taking her purse out, she had opened it and extracted a photo from a see through compartment.

The friend had then compared the screen photo and the photograph in her hands. She turned to the other women and pointed to both scenes.

The friend's shot showed a mid-teens smiling girl standing in front of some gates. In the background there were two sheds in what looked like an allotment. Both were painted red but one looked more faded than the other.

The three women examined the scenes and Anne's neighbour pointed to some trees and an embankment to the right of the sheds.

The same trees and embankment showed in both photos. The trees in the friend's print seemed slightly smaller but otherwise everything looked to be a match.

The only noticeable differences, apart from the girl, were the colours of the sheds and the fact that the larger pink one was on a different side. Otherwise everything from the foreground gravel, the gates and the overall scene was the same. Both taken from almost exactly the same position.

The girl in the picture was the friend's daughter who had left home about five years ago. There had been a heated mother/daughter argument about boyfriend suitability for a 15 year old and she had packed a few things and just left.

There had been no contact for two years until the photo just showed up in the post one morning. There was a message on the back saying she was well, was sorry and would phone soon to try to patch things up.

The envelope had a Coventry postmark but there was no other clue to where it had been sent from.

The promised phone call had never materialised and there had been no further contact.

The worried woman had initially contacted the police as soon as it was apparent that her daughter had indeed left home for good this time.

Although she was a minor and could be in danger, there really wasn't a lot they could do. They put her details on a Missing Person list and that was that.

The friend waited a suitable amount of time for the promised phone call from her daughter. Then she had contacted the police again and showed them the photo. Again, with no clue as to location, there was nothing they could do. The Missing Person list had drawn a blank.

Anne thought it was an incredible coincidence that two photos of almost the same scene had come together like that. It gave her goose bumps, she said.

She asked if it was ok for me to print off the picture from the Polish mother and show it around at the allotments? She had scanned it and included it with the other pictures.

Maybe one of the people down there had seen the missing woman at the allotments and knew where she currently lived.

I looked at both the pictures. There was no doubt that the scenes were the same. I sensed what Anne had said about goose bumps. What were the odds that two people with the same picture would meet each other by chance like that?

About the same as the time I was on the outskirts of Munich, Germany and offloading in a street. A car had stopped and the driver had got out to ask me for directions. He just happened to be my next door neighbour. So, yes, I knew that almost impossible co-incidences did sometimes happen.

I printed off the friend's picture in original form and then another tighter shot of just the girl's head.

I emailed Anne back saying that I would do what I could.

I had made up a poster and put it in the notice board by the main gates.

It was along the lines of "Have you seen this Polish person? Missing from home. Parents worried. Any information to...." and my plot number and home telephone number.

Rugby, like most other places in the UK, has a sizeable Polish population. Many come for the work available in the DIRFT warehousing complex. Others set up shop supplying familiar foods at unfamiliar prices.

I was working on my plot that afternoon when a guy stopped by. I had seen him about and knew he had a plot on the Lower End.

He introduced himself as Jan with a hawk and spit surname. He was Polish and had seen the missing girl around three years ago, he said. Her name was Kinga Sadlek and she was then seventeen.

At the time she was fairly regular at the Polish get togethers in a town pub. He had tried to chat her up but found out she was involved with someone. He would see her spasmodically in town or down the pub and they would chat.

She said she was living in Dunchurch with an older man. He suspected that he was also used her as a punch bag.

Several times he had seen her with visible injuries: a split lip, make up barely concealing a black eye and other bruises. From the way she held herself sometimes he thought there were less visible injuries.

Of course she had made out that the injuries were a result of a fall or carelessness. "Why do women do that?" he asked. "Why do they stay? Why live with a violent man?"

He also remembered that she had told him her man had an allotment somewhere in Rugby. She went with him sometimes to get vegetables or help on the plot.

I asked him if it was this allotment. "I don't know." He replied. "I have only been here for the last year. But it could have been."

I told him about the photos and that it was this allotment she had been photographed at. That seemed to upset him. I guess he had fancied her.

He had told her she should leave this man. Move somewhere else. His cousin lived in Leeds and she could stay with him and his family until she found a place to stay and a job, he had told her.

She thanked him and said she would think about it.

"Anyway, after a while, I stopped seeing her about and thought she had moved on. " Jan remembered.

The hairs on the back of my neck were already itching. When Jan had mentioned Kinga was living with an older man in Dunchurch I had almost instantly thought "Collins" for some reason. Another co-incidence or still the same one, only bigger?

When I got home I emailed Anne with my news and asked her if she could find out whether the missing girl's was Kinga Sadlek or not.

I told her that, even if it was the same person, there was still no clue to her whereabouts.

She later confirmed the name and asked me to keep trying. Something might turn up, she said.

Nothing did. Jan asked around the Polish community but no-one knew anything. The general consensus was that she had done the sensible thing and moved on.

26: The Allotment!

John Burns had waited for some reaction to the Quit Notice he had sent Albert Collins. He had been relieved when there wasn't any.

Now all that remained was to re-let the two plots. He had plenty of people waiting but decided to wait until the warmer weather before he allocated the two plots.

People were more enthusiastic viewing potential plots in the Spring than in the snow, ice and cold of Winter. He decided that he would send a team down first to make sure things were presentable.

The first thing they would have to do was get rid of the two sheds. He had been down to see them and there and then decided they would have to go. Who would want anything like that on their plot?

He would give Collins ample time to remove them himself but they were definitely going.

*****

Winter turned into Spring and the Victory Allotments began to come alive again.

Adrian Miles watched the scene from his kitchen window change daily. Through the winter months there had been little activity. Sometimes he saw Dave Williams walking around with his yappy little dog. He would go out and have a chat but they still skirted around The Sheds incident. They both agreed that the allotments without Collins would be a better place.

The Allotmenteers had met up a couple of times at Crick since. More for the chance to get out, have a drink and chat than for anything else.

The conversation inevitably turned to Collins at some point. The speculation as to where he was or doing was varied and inventive.

Big Mick has proposed that the group continue but more outside the allotments. Of course, he had been drinking but some of it made some sort of sense.

Still wrapped up in the romance and notion of the Allotmenteers' One for All and All for One philosophy, he had suggested that they become a Neighbourhood Watch, Street Vigilante, type group. Keeping the streets safe, fighting for the weak, that sort of thing.

He smiled as he remembered Big Mick, a few pints inside him, singing a parody of the Ghost Busters theme song "When you got a problem, who you gonna call? The Allotmenteers." in a slurred voice.

He was beginning to look more and more like the Marshmallow Man from the end of the Ghostbusters film.

The others laughing at, and with him. But, annoyingly, the stupid song kept repeating itself in his head on the way home.

The idea had some appeal though. The amount of vandalism, street crime, littering, dog crap and other annoyances that the council and police couldn't or wouldn't deal with was a joke. Except that it was no laughing matter.

The idea of a bunch of geriatric Charles Bronson type vigilantes roaming the night-time streets was much funnier.

But, Spring was well on the way and soon there would be little time for anything but his plot.

Dave, Paul and Big Mick would be getting new sheds, of varying size, material and condition to replace the ones destroyed by the fires. They would all help each other build them.

There would be new tenants coming and everyone on the allotments would need to make sure there would be no repeat of the Albert Collins' tyranny.

First sign of anyone getting overly uppity and everyone would. have to unite and fight it. Somehow he didn't think it would ever happen again. There was still a sense of group shame over what happened.

*****

The change from Winter to Spring was seamless. One minute I was all wrapped up against the cold and the next, it seemed, I was busy down the allotments again.

I had repaired the little damage that the snow had done to my fence and the plot was in good shape.

Another few warm days and it would be time to get the shovels and forks out.

Get the seeds planted and the whole yearly cycle would start again.

This time would be my first solo year so I was hoping for better results than the joint efforts of Geoff, Jane and myself.

The Boss still intended to involve herself but probably in a more supervisory and creative way.

I started calling her The Boss when she took exception to being called The Gangmaster.

Meanwhile I was putting the finishing touches to my new shed. It had arrived yesterday on the back of a pick-up. I had looked for a good second hand one but failed. In the end I had gone for new.

The Allotmenteers had helped me carry it up from the gate and erect it. It had only taken a few hours. Big Mick and Paul were in the process of building theirs.

Everyone on the site contributed wood, nails and other stuff and the results were coming along in a unique and unforgettable fashion.

Now I was just moving my stuff in. Bits and pieces from home and the tools I kept in Adrian's garage.

I put up a couple of shelves, a tool rack and things like that. A sturdy lock on the door. I loved the smell of the new timber.

The Boss had already insisted I take measurements for the new curtains she was thinking about running up. I couldn't wait.

Dotted about the allotments were the council men who had arrived in two vans and a truck earlier. Some were strimming the pathways.

Others were cutting down overhanging branches and some were just generally tidying up and trying to look busy.

Four of them were skillfully dismantling The Homo's Home, the smaller of the pink sheds, with sledge hammers and crow bars.

It only took a few minutes before there was a heap of splintered wood and ripped felt being loaded onto the flat bed truck.

Once that had been done, they turned their attentions to The Peedo Pad. First of all they removed any tools or flammable equipment and put them in a heap near the gates.

I was reminded of doing the same with the burnt remains from Geoff's shed.

Because this shed was bigger it took longer. First they lifted off the canted roof in two sections and stacked them by the gate. Then, one by one, the walls were unbolted and removed to the gates.

Finally, the four of them put a fork at each corner of the heavy floor section and lifted. As the floor was slowly lifted, each man grabbed hold and walked it to the gate.

One guy called to one of the crew using a chainsaw and he cut the floor, sides and roof sections into manageable pieces.

These were then loaded on to the truck. In less than an hour, all trace of the sheds had gone.

After a suitably long tea and fag break, two of the shed guys unloaded a rotovator from one of the vans and wheeled it over. One began to rotovate the smaller plot whilst the others offered helpful advice and criticism.

There is something enjoyable yet annoying seeing a rotovator at work. What would take back breaking work with a fork and spade is achieved in minutes mechanically. I watched as the rotovator guy started work on the bigger plot.

Not many of the tenants had them because of the cost although some did hire one at the start of the season for the heavy cultivating.

As I imitated the council workers and leant on my fork watching the mechanical marvel, I had the sudden brainwave of an equipment co-op.

Why not just have one joint rotovator, chainsaw, strimmer, mower or other item of specialized equipment and let everybody share the purchase cost and use?

I was idly mulling this over, searching for pros and cons, when there was a distraction from the main gates. The rotovator had stopped and the guy using it was doubled over and appeared to be retching. Had there been an accident?

His mates were hurrying over to see what the problem was. They all stood around the rotovator until one of them walked away and took out his mobile.

The others walked the rotovator man away. One of them went to a van and returned with a blue plastic sheet. He spread it out at the side of the rotovator. What was going on?

By now several of the other tenants had seen that something was happening and were walking over.

The guy who fetched the sheet must have been in charge because he was suddenly pointing and telling the others to stop anyone from going near the plot.

Then, within minutes it seemed, the whole thing went crazy. We heard rapidly approaching sirens and then a police car was speeding into the car park. Barely had the driver got out and reached the gate before another car had joined his in the park.

The first one went to the group of council men and spoke to the one apparently in charge. He pointed to the blue sheet and both policemen walked over, lifted the sheet, looked and came back.

One began talking into his radio. The other went to his car and returned with some cones and a roll of red and white tape. Within minutes the plot was cordoned off and people were being kept away.

Before long there was a couple of people in white overalls and carrying metal cases, walking into the allotments and being directed to the blue sheet.

I guess we have all watched enough CSI and similar programmes to know this was a forensic team. And that meant a crime scene.

And I was getting a scary feeling that the photo coincidence thing was spreading out even further.

More police arrived and they began to take our names and addresses. They wouldn't say what was up but there was now a white tent in place around the blue sheet and rotovator.

And, as all of us armchair detectives knew, that meant a body was involved.

And, we realised, the reason why the shed had been moved from one side of the plot to the other.

27: The Allotment!

The summer of 2014 seemed to drag and fly by simultaneously. On the allotment it was long and hot. Days of blistering heat, welcome showers and steady growth.

I tended to start work early, go home for a siesta and then return in the evening for another bit of pottering.

Mornings or evenings were magical places on the Victory allotments. In the morning, around 6.30, sitting outside my shed, drinking tea and listening to the birds was my favourite time.

I had found that you don't get as much sleep as you get older. I would have liked more sleep but, most mornings, I was wide awake at five.

There didn't seem much point just lying there so I would get up and Zak and I would walk down to the allotments. Kettle on, tea made and just sit and listen.

The evening were a time to relax and enjoy the lingering heat. The Boss liked the late afternoons and evenings. Painting was a new hobby and she both liked and was good at it.

She would sit behind her easel, paint and direct me at my work. Multi-tasking she called it. We both lost weight, got brown, ate healthier and saved money.

We –I use the term loosely – planted spuds, dug up spuds, ate spuds. Carrots, onions, cabbages, melons, peas, turnips, swedes….the list was endless. If there was a seed for it, it got planted.

The Boss tended to do the artistic stuff like poking a hole in the ground and dropping a seed in. I did the basic stuff like digging the raised beds, raking them, weeding, putting up nets, taking down nets.

It was hard constant work, for one of us at least, but it was addictive.

You put a tiny seed into a hole. You watered it, fussed over it and watched it grow. Later, you picked it, cooked it and ate it. Food you had created. How good was that?

It was enjoyable, rewarding and we both enjoyed both the peaceful and the quiet moments.

In fact, the Victory allotments were a haven of tranquility in an ever changing and noisier world. All the plots were taken and we were a hard working, harmonious group. We tended to help our neighbours and vice versa.

Big Mick didn't make much pretence of doing anything other than eat and put on weight. But at least he was supporting the local Greggs.

Peter and Paul kept their plots up to their usual good standard.

Adrian tended to come over and flaunt his white hair whenever Lynne was about.

I had floated the idea of an equipment co-op and it had met with mostly approval. We decided to start a fund and obtain the equipment we needed in time for next spring.

Some were against the idea because they all ready had the equipment. Others because they didn't like anything new. But we were getting there slowly.

*****

The bad part of that summer was the seemingly constant police and press presence. The taking of statements, photographs and the almost constant intrusion.

As we suspected, the police did find a body. The big shed plot was then dug and sieved all over as they kept searching. The smaller plot was worked over as well but thankfully, no more bodies were found.

The forensic report read out in court said the body was female, had been strangled and had been the subject of constant beatings as evidenced by the broken and fractured bones. She had been buried sometime within the last five years.

DNA from the body matched the sample from the former Seven Oaks bedroom of Kinga Sadlek. She would have been just twenty.

The police were grateful for the photos and the names I had given them. They had made her identification quick and easy.

As for Albert Collins, he had just vanished. The police found where he had traded in his old van. They knew the details of his new camper van. There was evidence of him getting on the Eurotunnel train to France. But then there was nothing else.

There was a warrant out for his arrest and Interpol were involved but he had seemingly vanished. However, they seemed confident that it was only a matter of time before he was found and placed in custody.

Kinga Sadlek's mother buried her daughter in the family plot in Poland. It wasn't the outcome she had hoped for. But at least she now knew where her daughter rested and was content with that.

John Burns never did re-let the plot where Kinga was found. Instead he asked us what we wanted to do with it. We had a meeting and the general consensus was for some sort of remembrance garden.

We all chipped in with money, materials and our labour. We united as a team and went to work.

We levelled the ground, turfed it and put a white wooden picket fence around it. We planted flowers around the fence.

We built a sturdy shelter with a bench in it that faced the allotments. There were solar powered lights around it.

It was an area of quiet and contemplation. We made it nice.

We put a little plaque on the wall so people didn't forget.

So that we didn't forget.

*****

The Allotmenteers? We still meet for a drink now and then in Crick. The locals had just started to speak to us so that was something.

Big Mick was still floating his idea for forming a Pensioner Power Vigilante group.

In the relaxed, sometimes very relaxed, atmosphere of the pub it sometimes seemed like a good idea

Maybe in the long dark winter months when we got bored we might do something.

Shove the dog crap that the owners didn't pick up through their letterboxes at night.

Scare the crap out of the local youths who were annoying the old folk with their litter, loud music, swearing and shouting.

We could follow the ring leader home and sing Vera Lynne songs outside his house. Tip the contents of rubbish bins in his garden. Turn an inebriated Big Mick loose on him.

The possibilities were endless.

"When you got a problem, who you gonna call? The Allotmenteers!"

Maybe.

Only not just yet.

But, you never know. It might just happen one day.

Be good or else.

You have been warned.

Author's Note.

Finally, it's finished. Done and dusted. The first of my books that isn't about trucks, trucking and my grand daughter Tilly Lee.

To separate the two topics, I write as Jethro Le' Roy -borrowed from Leroy Jethro Gibbs from NCIS - on the Allotmenteers books and Dave Furlong, my real name, on the others

The idea for this book came about when I got an allotment to try to deal with the boredom of retirement.

Some of it is true. Mostly it is fiction. I hope you enjoy it. If you do, could you write a review please?

Most authors welcome honest and constructive reviews as a guide to how they are doing.

Because, though I write mainly for my own enjoyment, (and to pass the time) I like to think that people do read and enjoy my books.

This is the planned first in a series of the Allotmenteers books.

You might want to try my books for Truckers and Children by Dave Furlong as well. You never know, you might like them.

You can find them all on Amazon in both paperback and Kindle versions.

Dave Furlong has been a truck driver, an owner operator and a transport journalist.

He has travelled extensively throughout the UK and Europe as both a truck driver and a journalist.

As a freelance journalist he has written articles and road tested new trucks for the major national and international transport and truck driver magazines.

He has also driven the many thousands of the miles involved in the rigorous manufacturer testing and development of new trucks , engines and drivelines.

He is now retired but continues to write about trucks and truckers under his Dave Furlong pen name.

The Allotment! is the first in his books about his allotment and the characters he meets down there.

38709667R00204

Printed in Great Britain
by Amazon